A gift for:

From:

Christmas 2025

Dear Friends,

The one question most authors are asked is: *Where do you get your ideas?*

For me it starts with something I've read or heard or seen. The plot for *A Ferry Merry Christmas* came when the local news reported that a Washington State Ferry traveling between Bremerton and Seattle had struck a sandbar. As a result, the passengers were stranded for hours until a tugboat came to their rescue.

That was all it took for my imagination to immediately overflow with what-ifs. What if it was Christmastime? What if there were compelling reasons people needed to get to Seattle? What if, on the other side of Puget Sound, there were friends or family eagerly anticipating their arrival? Instinctively, I recognized this real-life incident had the potential for a great story.

As an author I've learned there are some stories that almost write themselves, and others where each page feels as if I'd chiseled it in stone. This book was a sheer joy to write. My hope is that you will find that same pleasure reading it as I did in the writing. Now, turn the page and take a seat on the Washington State Ferry as it traverses the waterways of Puget Sound.

As always, I enjoy hearing your thoughts. You can reach me through all the social media platforms. If you'd rather use snail mail, my address is: P.O. Box 1458, Port Orchard, WA 98366.

From my family to yours, have a joyous and fun-filled holiday season.

Merry Christmas,

Debbie Macomber

P.S. Take heart, in all the years I've lived in the Seattle area, this is the only time I can remember a ferry hitting a sandbar.

BALLANTINE BOOKS FROM DEBBIE MACOMBER

Must Love Flowers
The Best Is Yet to Come
It's Better This Way
A Walk Along the Beach
Window on the Bay

Cottage by the Sea
Any Dream Will Do
If Not for You
A Girl's Guide to Moving On
Last One Home

ROSE HARBOR INN

Sweet Tomorrows
Silver Linings
Love Letters

Rose Harbor in Bloom
The Inn at Rose Harbor

BLOSSOM STREET

Blossom Street Brides
Starting Now

CHRISTMAS NOVELS

A Christmas Duet
The Christmas Spirit
Dear Santa
Jingle All the Way
A Mrs. Miracle Christmas
Alaskan Holiday

Merry and Bright
Twelve Days of Christmas
Dashing Through the Snow
Mr. Miracle
Starry Night
Angels at the Table

2 IN 1 COLLECTIONS

A Bright New Day:
Borrowed Dreams and *The Trouble with Caasi*

All Roads Lead Home:
A Friend or Two and *Reflections of Yesterday*

The Perfect Holiday:
That Wintry Feeling and *Thanksgiving Prayer*

What Matters Most:
Shadow Chasing and *Laughter in the Rain*

Tying the Knot:
Yesterday's Hero and *White Laces and Promises*

That Christmas Magic:
Christmas Masquerade and *The Gift of Christmas*

A Ferry Merry Christmas

DEBBIE MACOMBER

A Ferry Merry Christmas

A Novel

BALLANTINE BOOKS

NEW YORK

Ballantine Books
An imprint of Random House
A division of Penguin Random House LLC
1745 Broadway, New York, NY 10019
randomhousebooks.com
penguinrandomhouse.com

Copyright © 2025 by Debbie Macomber

Penguin Random House values and supports copyright. Copyright fuels creativity, encourages diverse voices, promotes free speech, and creates a vibrant culture. Thank you for buying an authorized edition of this book and for complying with copyright laws by not reproducing, scanning, or distributing any part of it in any form without permission. You are supporting writers and allowing Penguin Random House to continue to publish books for every reader. Please note that no part of this book may be used or reproduced in any manner for the purpose of training artificial intelligence technologies or systems.

BALLANTINE BOOKS & colophon are registered trademarks of Penguin Random House LLC.

Hardcover ISBN 978-0-593-97467-4
Ebook ISBN 978-0-593-97468-1

Printed in the United States of America on acid-free paper

1st Printing

First Edition

BOOK TEAM: Production editor: Jennifer Rodriguez
Managing editor: Pamela Alders • Production manager: Katie Zilberman
Copy editor: Amy Brosey • Proofreaders: Andrea Gordon,
Deborah Bader, Amy Harned

Book design by Sara Bereta

Adobe Stock illustrations:
FRESH TAKE DESIGN (anchor), Tasha (Christmas pattern)

The authorized representative in the EU for product safety and compliance is Penguin Random House Ireland, Morrison Chambers, 32 Nassau Street, Dublin D02 YH68, Ireland. https://eu-contact.penguin.ie

To
Doris LaPorte
and
Robert Hudson
Both of you are treasured by Wayne and me

A Ferry Merry Christmas

CHAPTER ONE

Avery Bond enjoyed studying people. A lot could be said about a person by simple observation. Her gaze floated over those waiting inside the Bremerton terminal for the *Yakima,* the ferry to Seattle.

Her attention landed on what appeared to be a young businessman who seemed to be in a hurry. He'd glanced at his watch twice in the last ten minutes as if anxious to board the ferry. She couldn't blame him. It was two days before Christmas, and she imagined he was eager to head to the city to be with his family. Her keen sense of observation was as active as her imagination was. She pictured said man on a quick trip across Puget Sound, looking to finalize a big business deal and promising his loved ones he'd be back in a flash. Perhaps the details had taken longer than he anticipated and now he was nervous, wanting to keep his word.

Avery's gaze moved to the grandmotherly woman in the seat just down from him. She found her interesting as well. The white-haired woman with the full-length beige wool coat had a large round tin box resting on her lap. The cheerful snowman design suggested it contained homemade cookies or candy that perhaps the maternal-looking woman had made herself. The way she held it firmly within her grip said that a lot of love and effort had gone into the preparation. Avery pictured decorated sugar cookies, thick with frosting and sprinkles, along with a layer of fudge and divinity. She could almost see the smiles of the woman's grandchildren when they discovered the special treats inside. What captured her attention was the dignified way in which she sat, as though she was comfortable with herself. Avery admired that.

A pang went through Avery's heart as she continued to study the woman. How desperately she missed her own grandmother. This would be her and Reed's first Christmas without their beloved Grams. Grams had raised them from the time they were five and eight. Their mother had gotten hooked on drugs and had deteriorated until the state had intervened and placed Avery and Reed with their grandparents. Over the years their mother made several attempts to get her life in order, but it never lasted more than a few months. Sadly, she was dead by the time she was thirty-three. Their father had never been in the picture, and when contacted by the state, he, too, was found unfit to raise Avery and her brother.

It couldn't have been easy for Grams and Gramps to take on two young kids. They never complained, and showered both children with love and guidance. Gramps went to be with the Lord ten years earlier, when Avery was fifteen. Reed had graduated from high school and was in his first year of college at the University of Washington.

Avery had always found order in numbers; they made sense to her. She'd gotten a degree in accounting and worked at a local firm in the Bremerton/Silverdale area. When her grandmother's cancer advanced to the point that she needed extra care, Avery had moved back home. Reed, who lived in Seattle, came to visit nearly every weekend until the end. They had both been at Grams's bedside, each holding a hand, as she peacefully passed from life to death.

When the will was read, they learned Grams had left the house to Reed and Avery. Because the home had been well maintained with a large, vibrantly colored flower garden, it sold quickly. Avery used her portion of the inheritance as a down payment for a one-bedroom condo close to her office. Reed had done the same, opting for a two-bedroom condo in the heart of downtown Seattle. Because he had the larger home, Avery planned to join him for Christmas.

Avery was proud of her brother. He'd done well for himself. With his degree in computer science, he'd been hired by Microsoft upon graduation and had quickly advanced in his career. Over the last year, he'd introduced her to two of his bachelor friends. Avery didn't appreciate his matchmaking efforts, although she understood her brother had her best interests at heart. Being three years older, Reed worried about Avery living alone, as she often worked late hours, especially during tax season. As far as she was concerned, it was about time for her brother, who recently turned twenty-nine, to settle down himself.

The ferry docked and the sound of the cars unloading was a clear indication that the boat was running on schedule. Those in the terminal were all walk-on passengers. From her position near the window, she was able to view the long line of vehicles waiting to board. The turnaround time was between fifteen and twenty minutes. Because of the Christmas holidays, the ferries were running at full capacity. Avery didn't envy the crew having to work this rainy, blustery day. Despite the high spirits and good cheer of the season, Seattle's drizzling, gray skies were as predictable as Santa's arrival Christmas Eve.

After a few minutes the announcement came that the walk-on passengers could proceed onto the ferry. People scurried ahead to claim the booths with tables next to the windows. Avery traveled often enough to be content with the theater-style seating in the middle of the vessel and was in no hurry, letting others surge ahead. The man with the briefcase was one of the first to board, as if he couldn't get on the ferry fast enough.

She was at the end of the line when another man—around her age, she guessed—rushed into the terminal and raced to the ticket booth. He didn't need to be wearing his uniform for her to suspect he was part of the military—sailor, she guessed. Having lived in the Bremerton area for most of her life, she thought the signs were obvious. The clean-cut look, and even the way he walked identified him as being part of the Navy. Bremerton was a Navy town, with a base and shipyard that dominated the Sinclair Inlet. In addition, the Bangor submarine base north of Silverdale also contributed to the large military presence.

The sailor wasn't hard on the eyes, either, she noted, and in fact was quite handsome. Close to six feet tall, and muscular, he moved with purpose. Her gaze lingered on him for several seconds and she wasn't alone in her admiration. He seemed to have captured the attention of nearly every woman who remained in the waiting area. With good reason. Though she had a hard time looking away and certainly appreciated his service and dedication to protecting the country, Avery had serious reservations when it came to dating men in the military.

One disastrous relationship had taught her painful lessons and gave her pause when it came to romantic entanglements with those kinds of guys.

Typically, Navy men were here today, gone tomorrow, sailing off into the sunset. The last thing she needed was a broken heart. Her best friend all through college had been burned, too. They'd both learned the hard way . . . although this guy gave her pause.

Her grandparents had made it clear that she wasn't to date any sailors until after she graduated from college. She knew they would have preferred her to concentrate on her studies before seriously dating anyone, especially a military man. But she hadn't heeded their advice. During her second year of college she'd fallen hard for Rick Murphy, a sailor, who spoke of undying love and commitment. When he'd gone to sea, she faithfully awaited his return, burying herself in her studies. At first he sent regular texts and emails, but those gradually tapered off. Naturally, Avery had her suspicions, which she rationalized, as she was too in love to lose faith. When her grandmother cautioned her, she made excuses for Rick, unwilling to believe he'd used and abandoned her. When his ship docked, she was at the pier eagerly waiting to welcome him back. Only she wasn't the only one looking for Rick. His wife was there as well, having flown in to surprise him.

Avery felt betrayed and stupid. Of course there'd been signs, all of which she'd chosen to ignore because she wanted to believe what they shared was real. That was the first time she'd fallen in love, but if this was what love felt like, then she was wary of giving it a second go.

Sick with disappointment, she decided then and there to guard her heart, especially when it came to a relationship with a military man. Grams worried about her and Reed, too, she knew. It was easy to make excuses for why she didn't date often. She was busy finishing school and working a part-time job as well. What she really needed was time for her heart to heal.

Her current social life was nearly nonexistent. Her time had been absorbed in caring for her grandmother in the final year of Grams's life. During tax season it was impossible to even think about finding a relationship, as work consumed nearly every waking hour. But Reed was right. It was time for her to get back out there, and she would soon.

The sailor joined her at the end of the walk-on passenger line. "Merry Christmas," he greeted, coming to stand behind her.

Avery turned her head, and smiled. "Merry Christmas."

"I'm grateful I made the ferry," he added, apparently wanting to continue the conversation.

Avery smiled again, wondering if it was a good idea to encourage him. He seemed friendly enough, and she appreciated the effort—but her natural reserve convinced her to remain silent. If she did jump back into the dating scene, she wasn't sure she should start with someone serving in the Navy.

The line moved forward.

"I'm meeting my sister," he added, when she didn't respond. "I haven't seen her in over two years."

He didn't give up easily, she noticed.

"Between her schedule and mine, we've had a hard time connecting. What about you?" he asked, noting the carry-on suitcase she pulled along behind her. "Off to see some guy?"

Well, that was hardly subtle. He clearly wanted to know if she was involved. "As a matter of fact, yes."

"Oh." He sounded deflated.

Avery smiled to herself. No need to let him know her Christmas plans involved her brother.

"I recently transferred from the East Coast. It's the first shore leave I've had in twelve weeks."

Avery said what he likely heard often. "Thank you for your service."

They entered the ferry, and she headed for the seating in the middle of the passenger deck. Hoping to signal that she had no interest and wasn't keen to continue the conversation, she said, "I hope you have a good visit with your sister."

"Ah, thanks . . ."

Avery took a seat in the front row. It looked like the sailor was about to ignore her parting shot and claim the seat next to her when someone called out for his attention.

"Harry, over here."

So his name was Harry. She had to admit she was mildly interested and flattered by his attention; however, the timing wasn't the best with the holidays upon them.

Harry paused and explained as if she needed this information. "Those are a few of my shipmates. Save a seat for me, will you?"

"Actually, I . . ." He was already out of earshot before she could suggest that he sit with his friends.

She had just taken her seat when a little girl of around five or six jumped into the chair next to her.

"Hello," Avery said, surprise lifting her voice.

"Hello." She had on a red coat, with her long pigtails hitting the top of her shoulders. She swung her legs, crossing her ankles, showing off her missing two front teeth. "I'm Olivia and my mom is taking me to visit Santa."

"Are you going to tell him what you want for Christmas?" Avery asked, remembering her own visits to Santa as a child.

Olivia nodded eagerly. "I want an iPad like my friends have so I can play games and draw and learn stuff."

"You must be a smart girl."

"I am," she returned with pride. "Both my teacher and my mommy tell me that all the time. But I could be even smarter if I had an iPad. Do you have one? Lots of people do. My mommy has one. She lets me play with hers sometimes, but it isn't the same as having my own."

The little girl chatted away as her mother took the seat beside her daughter. "Sorry," she said. "Is Olivia talking your ear off?"

"Mommy, don't be silly. No one can talk off anyone's ear."

A Ferry Merry Christmas 13

"I know, love. That is a nice way of asking if you were pestering her."

Olivia instantly looked offended. "Was I being a pest?" she asked Avery.

"Not in the least," Avery assured both mother and daughter. "Olivia was telling me she's visiting Santa this afternoon and wants to let him know what the biggest desire of her heart is for this Christmas."

Olivia turned to look at Avery. "It's all right to let my mommy know what it is. I've already told her."

"Like a thousand times," the mother murmured under her breath. "I'm Beth, by the way."

"Avery," she returned.

"That's a pretty name," Olivia said. "No one in my class has that name."

"I like it, too," Avery returned.

Olivia's feet continued to sway as the ferry's engine came to life and the boat started to pull away from the Bremerton dock.

After a few moments, Olivia said, "I really need to talk to Santa, though."

"That's why we're visiting him," her mother assured her.

"But I want more than an iPad."

Beth caught Avery's eyes and blinked as if this was news to her.

"Have you been a good girl?" Avery asked Olivia.

"Oh yes, I've been especially good this year."

Avery had to smile. She was about to say more when a group of four men and one woman entered the cafeteria, climbing up the stairs from the car deck. One of them carried a guitar, and Avery surmised they were members of a band. They headed to the long line at the small cafeteria and Avery was able to hear smidges of their conversation.

"Our first paying gig . . ."

"We got this. It's only up from here."

"Suzie, keep your throat lubricated so you're fresh . . ."

Olivia tugged at her sleeve and Avery realized the little girl was trying to get her attention again. Leaning down so Olivia could whisper in her ear, the little girl said, "I need Santa to know what I really want for Christmas is my daddy to come home."

Avery's heart ached for her. Beth seemed to have heard her daughter and her face went tight, as if she was struggling to hide her emotion.

Avery was saved from having to address the issue when her phone chirped. Caller ID showed the call as coming from Reed.

"Excuse me, Olivia, this is my brother calling."

"Okay," she said graciously, as if granting Avery permission to answer.

"Merry Christmas, big brother," she said.

"You're on the ferry?"

"Yup. I should arrive around twelve-thirty. The ferry arrived on schedule, so I should be in Seattle on time."

"Great. I thought I'd walk to the dock and greet you. My condo is less than six blocks from there."

His thoughtfulness was something of a surprise. "No need to do that."

Reed ignored her objection. "I plan on treating you to lunch."

Avery was instantly suspicious. This could well be another matchmaking attempt. "Just the two of us?"

"Funny you should ask that—"

"Reed," Avery cut him off. "I prefer to find my own dates, thank you very much."

"I know, and agree, however, Sam is a great guy. The least you can do is meet him."

"Over lunch, with my brother listening in on every word? No, thanks. Call him right now and explain that I would prefer to wait for a more convenient time." *Like never,* she mused.

"You sure?"

"I'm positive. Although, thinking about it, I would

enjoy being treated to lunch by my big brother. I'm hungry. I skipped breakfast this morning. All I ask is that you make sure it's a table for two, not three."

"Message received."

"Where is the reservation?" Her brother had taken her to a wonderful seafood restaurant recently, and she was eager to return.

"Anthony's."

"Perfect. You couldn't have chosen better."

"I made those reservations shortly after our last time there."

"That was in October. You mean to say it's been on the books that long?" Surprise showed in her voice. She knew it would be difficult to reserve a table this close to Christmas, since Anthony's, part of a local chain, was extremely popular.

Their lunch in the fall had been a birthday treat. It was the first year her grandmother hadn't been alive to cook Avery's favorite dish of seafood spaghetti. Reed had done his best to help her through the sadness of missing Grams. Her brother was kind like that. He thought ahead and took the initiative, which was one reason he'd advanced as quickly as he had in his career with Microsoft.

"I asked for a table by the window."

A Ferry Merry Christmas 17

"Reed, that's so nice. I can't wait, and I promise, hungry as I am, not to order half the menu."

"It's Christmas. Order whatever you want."

Avery ended the conversation with a huge smile. Although Grams was gone, at least they had each other and would make the best of things, as they always had.

CHAPTER TWO

Harrison Stetler glanced longingly at the woman he'd chatted with while boarding the ferry. She didn't appear overly receptive, but he hoped with a bit of gentle persistence he could persuade her to give him a chance. They'd be on the ferry for nearly an hour, and that was enough time to get to know each other a little bit. She'd mentioned she was meeting some guy. Normally that would be enough for Harrison to look elsewhere. Nevertheless, she intrigued him, and given the chance, he'd like to talk to her more.

For reasons he couldn't explain, he wasn't sure he believed her about this other guy. He'd wanted to sit with her and test his theory. She was beautiful, and after three months at sea, he was hungry for connection. He was also new to the area and looking to make friends. He'd liked her immediately, although he couldn't say why. There was just something about her.

"Come on, Hairy," his buddy said while jabbing him in the ribs. His fellow seamen insisted on calling him Hairy, a play on his given name and the fact that his chest was, well . . . hairy.

"What?" he asked, hiding his frustration.

"Stop looking at that woman."

Feeling guilty, Harrison looked away. Also fresh on leave, Dan was happily married and heading to Seattle to meet up with his wife and one-year-old son, who were already at Dan's parents' home awaiting his arrival.

"You haven't taken your eyes off her once," Dan pointed out.

Harrison didn't realize he'd been that obvious.

"What's her name?"

Harrison sighed his disappointment. "I didn't get a chance to find out."

Dan mumbled something Harrison didn't catch.

"What was that?" he asked, tearing his eyes away from the pretty girl. Damn, he hadn't even gotten her name. Seeing she was sitting next to the woman with the little girl, it was highly unlikely that he'd get a chance now.

"Nothing important," Dan said.

Despite being caught, Harrison continued to study her. Her lack of interest didn't surprise him. At his last duty station on the East Coast, he'd discovered that a lot of local women were leery of dating men in the military. It made sense that the same reluctance applied to single women on the West Coast. He wasn't a player, although he knew plenty who were.

"Did you meet your wife while stationed here?" he asked Dan, hoping to get the lay of the land.

"No, we were teenage sweethearts. Julia and I dated all through high school."

Harrison had spent three months with the crew. A lot of the men kept their personal lives private, and Harrison wasn't one to pry. He didn't know Dan that well, and hesitated before he asked, "What did Julia think when you enlisted?"

"She was all for it," Dan replied without hesitation. "The benefits were too good to ignore. I'll complete my four years with another four in the reserve. With that commitment, I'll be able to get my college paid for, along with a housing stipend. It was the only way I could get my teaching degree without taking on the burden of student loans. Besides, we wanted to start a family right away and the Navy offered medical benefits."

"You should work for the recruitment program," Harrison joked.

Dan shook his head. "Naw, that's not my style. I like my work duties just fine. Three months under the sea and three months on land. I'm happy where I am, thank you very much."

Kyle, another of his shipmates, wandered over to where Harrison and Dan sat. He carried a large cup of coffee and a donut with him. "What's up?" he asked, sitting down with his friends.

"Hairy's looking for a love connection with a woman he saw walking onto the ferry."

Harrison rolled his eyes, letting Kyle know Dan was grossly exaggerating. Although to be fair, he was a bit annoyed that he'd lost the opportunity when his friends had called him away.

"I thought you were off to see your sister," Kyle said, and took a huge bite of the donut, washing it down with his coffee.

"I am." Harrison was looking forward to seeing Kellie more than he'd like to admit. They hadn't been close in their teens. Older by two years, Kellie was bossy and had always been very competitive. She'd gotten better grades than Harrison and she'd constantly rubbed it in. They'd argued endlessly. But once she left for college, their relationship changed for the better. He'd missed her hassling him, even if she was headstrong and opinionated.

In retrospect, Harrison had to admit Kellie was spot-on about his lack of initiative. He hadn't applied himself in high school and was more interested in sports and girls than he was in schoolwork. His senior year he'd had to buckle down and was fortunate to accumulate the credits he needed to graduate. Because of his poor grades and bad attitude, his parents weren't willing to pay for him to attend college, which prompted Harrison to enlist in the Navy.

In contrast to Harrison's failed teen years, Kellie had graduated from both high school and college with honors. Because of her academic excellence, and with a business degree in hand, she was promptly hired by Microsoft. Harrison was proud of her accomplishments and regretted the years they'd been at odds.

As adults, Harrison and Kellie were closer now than ever. They emailed and texted often. Spending Christmas with her gave him the opportunity to let her know how terrific he thought she was. He looked forward to having time together in person, which was an all-too-rare opportunity. Plus, he knew Kellie needed a bit of cheering up.

"Kellie's a hotshot executive with Microsoft," he boasted to his friends.

"Bet she's loaded."

"I wouldn't know. Since I was previously stationed in Maine, I haven't seen my sister in nearly two years." Any leave Harrison had, he'd spent visiting his parents and connecting with old friends. It worked out this year with him now stationed in Washington that he could visit Kellie. His parents were on a Christmas cruise with their best friends, sailing somewhere in the Caribbean islands, content that their two children would be together over the holidays.

"Cool," Dan said, and took another sip of his coffee.

"What are you doing for Christmas?" Dan asked Kyle.

"I have an aunt and uncle in Seattle, and they invited me to spend Christmas with them. My parents are driving over from Spokane and should arrive around the same time as I do. I haven't seen my two younger sisters in months."

"I didn't know you had sisters," Harrison commented.

"Hey, don't get any ideas. Sally and Ruth are too young for you."

"How young is too young?" Harrison asked, egging on his friend.

"Thirteen and fifteen."

"Yup," Harrison agreed. "Too young." However, the woman chatting with the little girl in pigtails with missing front teeth was exactly the right age. He shrugged off his thoughts. His philosophy was if it was meant to be, then it would happen. If they were to run into each other another time, then all the better. Clearly today wasn't the day.

He took out his phone and sent a text to Kellie.

I made the 11:45 ferry in the nick of time. Once in Seattle I'll Uber on up to your place.

Her response came back almost immediately.

As it happens, I'm in town, finishing up my Christmas shopping. I've got my car parked and will walk down to the ferry terminal and meet you there.

Great. That would save him the hassle of booking an Uber, which he feared might be difficult this close to Christmas. His sister lived in the Kirkland area. She'd mentioned in an earlier text that it could take as long as forty minutes to get from Seattle to Kirkland by car, as the traffic was bound to be heavy.

Christmas shopping? he texted back. *Find anything for your handsome younger brother?*

You wish. Did you happen to ship me any lobsters from Maine?

You're out of luck. Harrison chuckled. His sister's favorite seafood was lobster. He'd had one shipped to her for her birthday last April. She'd been over the moon. He knew it had helped soften the breakup with the guy she'd been dating for the last couple years. Jude—Harrison called him Judas—hadn't been willing to commit, and Kellie thought it highly unlikely the guy would change his mind. Harrison had the feeling that once Kellie broke off the relationship, Jude would realize his mistake and have a change of heart. Instead, Jude had started dating another woman almost immediately. The last update Kellie sent explained that Jude was now living with his new girlfriend. It'd been an awkward situation, because Kellie and Jude both worked in the same department. Kellie swore she'd never date a man who worked with her again. Harrison didn't blame her. She seemed wary now, and as far as he knew, she wasn't dating anyone currently.

That's what I thought. No lobster for me. See you soon.

Soon, he texted back.

"Hey, guys, you hear that?" Kyle sat up, as if detecting that something wasn't right.

"Hear what?" Harrison asked.

Kyle had twisted his head to one side, as if intently listening. His friend worked at the sonar station of their *Virginia*-class nuclear-powered submarine. Having a keen sense of hearing was only one of the reasons he was great at his job.

"I don't hear anything," Dan said. As if to discover what had gotten Kyle's attention, Dan squinted and appeared to strain to identify any difference in the sound. After a couple moments, he shook his head, letting Kyle know he didn't have a clue what his friend was talking about.

"The engine is slowing," Kyle said.

"You're imagining things," Dan said dismissively.

Harrison wasn't about to quibble with the guy who had the hearing of a bat. "I can't tell that there's a difference, but I wouldn't dismiss anything Kyle says."

One of the crew members walked past, and Kyle tried to grab his attention. The crewman wore a thick coat and knit cap that identified him as such. The name embroidered on his front was Earl Jones.

"Excuse me," Kyle called out.

Earl Jones paused alongside them, looking mildly irritated at the interruption.

"Can I ask you a question?" Kyle said.

"Sure thing. What can I do for you?" Earl asked, looking down at the cup of coffee he'd apparently recently purchased. Harrison knew if the guy manned the car deck that the winds must be bitter cold. His lips looked chapped, and he didn't seem elated to be working during the holidays, when the ferry traffic was at its peak.

"Are we experiencing engine troubles?" Kyle asked.

The crewman snickered as though he found the question amusing. "What makes you think that?"

"The engine sound is different from when we left Bremerton."

Earl Jones all but rolled his eyes. "What are you, some kind of mechanical engineer?"

Harrison took offense to his attitude. "No, Kyle is a sonar expert; he knows his business. You might want to let someone know."

"I'll get right on that," the other man returned flippantly and walked away.

Harrison looked out the window. Kyle wasn't making this up. While Harrison hadn't heard anything, he did notice that the ferry had slowed. He glanced at the time and was surprised to see they were already a half-hour into the sailing. "Shouldn't we be closer to Seattle by now?" he asked. From this vantage point, the city should clearly be in view, and it was still much farther in the distance than it should be.

"What did you say?" A businessman sitting across from them leaped to his feet. He stared at Harrison, looking for an answer. "Should we be closer to docking than we are?" He nervously rubbed his hands together.

"According to the schedule, we should be docking at one-thirty and it's nearly one now. I don't usually take this ferry, so I'm unsure of exactly where we should be in Puget Sound at this point, but it seems we're still a good distance away."

The businessman left his briefcase behind as he hurriedly walked to the back of the passenger deck to the doors that led outside. A few brave souls lined the railing, letting the wind whip around them. Seagulls circled overhead. A light snow-rain combination swirled about, carried by the breeze.

Within a couple minutes the businessman returned, his nose red from the cold. He rubbed his hands together, trying to warm them. "I talked to someone who takes this ferry several times a week and he said we should be way closer to Seattle by now. What's going on?" he demanded.

"I haven't got a clue," Harrison told him, although he wasn't sure the other man was looking for a response.

All at once there was a jolt and the ferry went completely dead in the water.

"We've stopped moving," Dan said, as if he were the only one who'd noticed.

Nearly everyone on the passenger deck was on their feet and looking out the window, wondering what the problem could be.

The same crewman who'd been sarcastic earlier returned and was immediately hit with a barrage of questions. A cacophony of noise filled the room as the passengers demanded answers.

Raising his arms to quiet the crowd, Earl Jones spoke. "No worries, folks. These things happen from time to time. We'll be on our way shortly."

"Are you sure about that?" someone from the back shouted.

"Of course," the crewman claimed dismissively. "These ferries run like clockwork."

"Then what's the holdup?" someone else asked.

He sighed, as if having to explain these matters was a drain on his energy. "It could be any number of things. The captain might have spotted a pod of orcas."

The older woman who sat close to the little girl in pigtails dismissed that idea: "Not this time of year."

"If there's an abandoned vessel in the water, the captain is required to report it in case someone is in the water."

A murmur of dissension followed.

"Could one of the crew have fallen overboard?" came another question.

"That's highly unlikely."

"But possible?"

Earl shrugged.

Leaning back with his arms folded, Kyle said loud enough for everyone to hear, "Could it possibly be engine trouble?"

The crewman glared at Kyle. "No way. The engines on these ferries are the best in the world."

No sooner had he finished speaking than the loudspeaker squeaked, indicating a forthcoming announcement.

"Ladies and gentlemen, this is Captain Douglas. I apologize for the delay. We are currently experiencing engine problems. Our team is investigating the issue. As soon as I have an update, I'll let you know. For now, sit back and relax. Hopefully the issue will be resolved quickly."

After the announcement ended, it seemed that everyone started to talk at once, voices of discontent filling the area as folks expressed their dissatisfaction.

"I told you we should have driven around," Harrison heard a woman bitterly complain to her husband.

"I'll be late for our family party," another complained.

"Join the club," Dan commiserated. "My wife and son are already at my aunt's place along with my parents."

"I've got to get to work," someone else shouted. "I need this job."

"No, no," the businessman said and groaned, "this can't be happening." He placed his hands over his face and bent in half, resting his forehead on his knees.

Harrison knew that whatever the reason, the delay must be more than a casual inconvenience for this guy.

CHAPTER THREE

After the captain's announcement, Virginia Talbot's fellow passengers headed for the cafeteria. They apparently weren't willing to second-guess the length of the delay.

She was grateful she'd eaten earlier, although not much. This trip into Seattle was long overdue. It'd been two years since she'd last talked to her sister. They'd had a disagreement over their parents' estate, and instead of settling it like civilized women, they'd argued to the point that they no longer communicated beyond a few terse text messages or emails.

Once they'd been as close as any twin sisters could be, caring for their aging parents, dealing with the aftermath of their deaths, each grieving. Dad had been thoughtful in the financial decisions, making sure the estate had been evenly divided between them. His goal was to eliminate any potential problems.

What he hadn't anticipated was the disagreement over Mom's china. It had been a wedding gift and used only for special occasions. As the oldest, Virginia felt she should take the twelve place settings and Veronica could have the silverware. The silverware was by far the more valuable of the two.

Instead, Veronica had insisted she should have the china and had no interest in the silverware. Earlier, Virginia had given in on Mom's pearls, letting Veronica have those when she had always admired them. Veronica knew Virginia would treasure those pearls. It was a power play to her, making sure Virginia got only what Veronica thought was right.

Hoping to keep the peace, Virginia had agreed to let her twin have the pearls. She got her mother's ruby ring instead. Although she'd yearned for the pearls, she'd been determined to be content with this special gift from the estate.

When it came to the china, though, she put her foot down. The china rightly belonged to her, and this time she wasn't giving in. The sole reason her sister wanted it was because Virginia had said she did. This time she refused to bend. Veronica made a huge fuss, complaining to any and all who'd been willing to listen about how she'd been cheated.

The bad feelings escalated from there. At one point, sick of arguing, Virginia offered up half of the twelve place settings in exchange for half of the silverware. Veronica wasn't interested. With her it was all or nothing.

If Veronica chose nothing, then that suited Virginia just fine. So nothing was what she got. The silence between them was deafening. Tragic. Sad.

As time passed, Virginia felt the loss of the close relationship she'd once shared with her sister. It hurt when their shared birthdays passed without a word from either. Holidays were the same. They'd always spent Christmas together, even as young newlyweds.

Their parents would be upset if they ever knew a twelve-place setting of china was what drove this wedge between them. Thankfully, they would never know, and for that Virginia would always be grateful.

Someone had to make a move toward reconciliation. This silence was a thorn in Virginia's side, an ache she couldn't relieve. She'd been a widow long before she lost her father and then a year later her mother. Her children all lived in the Kitsap Peninsula and visited often. They were a close family.

This Christmas, however, both of her children would be away. Will had plans to spend the holidays with his in-laws. His family flew to the East Coast to be with Tamera's parents. It was only fair, as they hadn't seen her side of the family in nearly two years. They had dinner together a week earlier to celebrate and opened their gifts.

It came as a surprise when her daughter, Whitney, announced that her family had decided to take a ski trip to Whistler over Christmas. When Whitney realized Virginia would be alone, she invited her mother to join them. Virginia had no interest in skiing and even less in being away from home over the holidays.

It felt as if God was telling Virginia it was time for her to make peace with her twin. For days she struggled with how best to reach out to Veronica. A letter would be more personal, or even a phone call. She debated both and found fault with each. She feared Veronica might not answer if she knew Virginia was on the other end of the line. Nor would she know if her sister took the time to read a letter.

In the end, she decided on a simple text.

She toyed with the wording for days, looking for a subtle approach without exposing her heart.

Veronica, do you happen to have Mom's recipe for her Christmas gingerbread cookies?

She already had the recipe; they both did. Her twin was sure to know this request had more to do with their relationship than with cookies.

Waiting for a response was nerve-racking. Two interminable days passed before Veronica replied. Virginia had to grit her teeth, knowing Veronica had taken the time to make her squirm. A dozen times she regretted making the effort when it was clear her sister, her identical twin, wasn't interested in a reconciliation. She'd swallowed her pride, and this was what she got.

By the time Veronica responded, Virginia had decided she'd made a terrible mistake. Her sister's answer was short and to the point.

Of course. Would you like it?

Please, she returned.

Within the hour her sister had supplied the list of ingredients and baking instructions.

Virginia took the next step, holding her breath the entire time she typed out the question.

I've been in a baking mood lately. I could make a double batch. Would you like some?

Veronica replied to her only a day later rather than two. Virginia took the faster response as promising. This was headway, however small.

I haven't done any baking this season. I would enjoy a batch of Mom's Christmas cookies.

That was all that was said. Virginia spent the better part of two days baking gingerbread cookies, frosting and decorating each one in the hopes that these cookies would work a miracle. A healing miracle between two sisters who had once been more than twins; they'd been best friends.

Once the cookies were prepared, Virginia sent another text. Again, she struggled with the wording.

I'm afraid the gingerbread cookies are too fragile to mail.

That left it open for Veronica to either collect the cookies or invite Virginia to deliver them. The choice would be hers.

Three days passed before she got a reply.

Could you deliver?

Okay.

She didn't say how pleased she would be to see Veronica again or anything else to indicate she was looking to make peace. To her way of thinking, Veronica needed to give her an indication she was willing to let bygones be bygones.

Eventually they'd set the date for December 23. After checking the weather forecast for the day, Virginia chose to take the ferry. Temperatures were dipping and there was a chance of black ice. Driving in the city was intimidating enough. She considered herself wise to hop on the ferry and take an Uber to her sister's home on Capitol Hill.

Even though she'd caught the early ferry, giving herself plenty of time, it seemed unlikely she would be there at their agreed-upon time.

With some hesitancy, she felt it necessary to update Veronica on the possibility of a delay.

I might be a little late, she typed.

Veronica texted right back.

How late?

I can't say for sure. She typed and was about to mention she was on the ferry when her twin's response flashed across the screen.

I have plans for later, so I'll need to know exactly how late you intend to be.

Virginia should have known her sister would make this difficult.

With her lips tight, she typed once again, her finger punctuating each letter to the point that her fingernails bent with the action.

As I said, I won't know that until later.

Then perhaps it would be best if you didn't come.

Virginia rolled her eyes before she typed the question.

Is that what you want?

Silence as deafening as the two years in which they hadn't spoken. Loud and sad. So very sad.

CHAPTER FOUR

At the captain's announcement, Avery reached for her phone to update her brother.

There's a problem with the ferry. Think it might be the engine, from what the captain said. The ferry stalled in the middle of Puget Sound. I'll update you as soon as we learn how long the delay will take.

Reed's response came only a few seconds later.

I hope everything's okay. The ferries rarely have trouble, so I'm sure you'll be along soon.

Avery returned her phone to her purse and checked the time. While her brother sounded hopeful, she had serious doubts she'd make their lunch. That was a minor disappointment. She appreciated her brother's thoughtfulness, knowing their time together was his way of helping her through the loss of their grandmother.

"Will I still see Santa Claus?" Olivia, the girl with pigtails who sat next to Avery, asked her mother. Her sweet, young face tightened with concern.

"There's still plenty of time to see Santa," Beth assured her daughter. Her gaze connected with Avery's, and she added in a nearly silent whisper, "I hope."

"The thing with Santa," Avery felt obliged to add, "is that he already knows you want an iPad for Christmas."

"But how can he, unless I tell him?" Olivia objected.

"He just does. Remember, not every little girl or boy has a chance to meet with Santa personally. Some write letters and others tell their parents and then the moms clue in Santa."

Olivia sighed with relief. "That's good to know."

Beth cast Avery an appreciative glance.

"Although," Olivia added, "I'd feel better if I could tell him myself."

"Of course you would," Avery agreed.

She noticed a lengthy line had formed heading into the small cafeteria. Not knowing how long the delay might take, she decided it was a good idea to grab a snack. In her rush to get to the ferry, she had skipped breakfast, and her stomach protested with a rumbling growl.

"Since we don't know how much time this is going to take, I'm going to buy a snack. Would you like me to grab something for you?" she asked Beth.

"No, thanks, we're good."

Leaving her overnight bag behind, Avery reached for her purse and stepped to the back of the queue. Immediately she was joined by the seaman she'd met on her way onto the ferry.

"Hey, we meet again," he said.

Not wanting to encourage him, Avery didn't respond and moved forward with the line.

"My shipmate noticed something wasn't right early on, even before the boat stopped moving." He continued making conversation. "Personally, I don't mind the delay, except my sister is waiting for me at the terminal. I hate holding her up."

"My brother is there, too," Avery said without thinking. And accidentally letting him know the man in her life was her brother. Her attention had been on the display case in the cafeteria. She noticed the prepared packaged sandwiches and clam chowder had sold out. The hot dogs went next. At this rate, the cafeteria would be completely empty by the time she got to the front of the line. She'd be lucky to find anything more than a bag of popcorn.

"So, this guy you're meeting is your brother?"

Now the sailor sounded downright gleeful, and she had no one to blame but herself. If she hadn't been thinking about her stomach, she wouldn't have offered up the information. Sometimes she didn't know where her head was.

"I'm Harrison," he said next, as the line slowly advanced.

Harrison, not Harry. *Interesting.*

"I didn't catch yours."

She turned to face him. "I didn't offer it," she told him, "but since you asked, it's Avery."

"Pleased to meet you."

Despite herself, she found him both charming and cute. "You, too. However, you should know I don't date men in the military."

"Is it a hard-and-fast rule based on personal experience?"

"Something like that," she admitted. "You know what they say, burned once, twice shy."

"In other words, some other guy broke your heart and you're hesitant. I get it."

"Not just some guy, some *Navy* guy."

"Ah," he said, as if it all made sense now. "So you're

holding all us Navy guys responsible for whatever this jerk did?" he asked, frowning. "I can't say I blame you, but don't you think it's unfair to color every man in the military as a loser because of one bad experience?"

"Perhaps, but it is what it is," she offered, which wasn't much of an excuse.

"I'm sorry that happened to you."

"No need to apologize. It wasn't your fault."

"Then give me a chance."

Avery mulled over her options. He had a point. "You seem like a perfectly nice person—"

"I am. Ask my shipmates if you want. As for sailors having a girl in every port, that's not me. It never has been, and it never will be. Unfortunately, it looks like you are unlikely to find out for yourself, which is a shame, because I think you're lovely, and I'd like to know you better."

Compliments weren't going to persuade her. Rick had been verbose with his praise, claiming she was the most beautiful girl he'd ever met; he couldn't take his eyes off her. "Thank you, but—"

He interrupted her again. "I have an idea. You can reject it if you want."

"And I likely will, but feel free." She gestured for him to continue.

"The ferry is dead in the water, right?"

"Right," she agreed.

"It could start up again at any time. It could be ten minutes, or it could be an hour. I'd like to suggest we have a conversation for however long it takes for the ferry to reach Seattle. No commitment, no pressure—a simple conversation. You can ask me anything you'd like.

"When we reach Seattle, we'll both go our separate ways, if that's what you want. If you feel comfortable enough to trust me, then great, even better. The choice will be completely up to you. How does that sound?"

Avery studied him for a moment. Likely the delay would last only a short while. She hated to admit how tempted she was. He was right, it was unfair to blame him for what Rick did. She should have learned her lesson. Should know better, but still . . .

Her pause encouraged him. "Who knows, I could be the man of your dreams."

"Ha." She laughed. "I see you've got a sense of humor."

"Come on, give me a chance."

She hesitated, looking at his undeniably handsome face, his well-defined cheekbones and the twinkle in his deep brown eyes. It would be far too easy to be swayed by his strong masculine appeal.

"Come on, Avery, what do you say? It could only be a few minutes and then you'll be free of me forever, if that's what you decide."

"And if I don't agree?" she asked.

He was quick to answer. "Then you can spend the rest of your life wondering if you passed up the chance of a lifetime."

Avery couldn't help it, she laughed again. "Okay, okay, we can chat for as long as it takes the ferry to reach Seattle. When we dock, though, the decision is mine and mine alone."

"You got it." He held out his hand and the two shook on it. "You won't regret this, I promise."

"That remains to be seen," Avery said, and hoped she wasn't making a mistake. She had to admit, though, he put up a good argument and she was tempted. His interest felt good, even if this was never going to go anywhere.

Her head shouted that this could be foolishness on her part, and at the same time her heart was busy telling her a short conversation wouldn't hurt. And once the ferry docked, they could each get on with their lives as if this interlude had never happened.

They reached far enough into the cafeteria to realize nearly all the food items had been purchased.

"It doesn't look like there will be much of a choice left," she commented. With every step Avery moved forward, the food options disappeared from the display cases.

"I noticed a vending machine with chips earlier. I'll check to see what's available there. Can I get you anything?"

The vending machine looked like it might be all there was, if that, too, hadn't been depleted.

"Okay, only I want to pay for it." She started to dig inside her purse when Harrison stopped her with a hand on her elbow.

"Wait. Let's see if anything is left first."

"Okay." That made sense, although she wanted it understood she didn't want to owe him.

"If there's a choice, what would you like?" he asked.

"At this point, I'll take whatever is left." She didn't hold out much hope, as the offerings at the cafeteria looked as bare as Old Mother Hubbard's cupboard.

Harrison disappeared around the corner and Avery eased her way to the cashier. When she reached the front of the line, she discovered that the only item left for sale was a small bag of popcorn. "I'll take it," Avery said, grateful for that.

"I'd pop more, but this is the last batch. We were scheduled to load up on supplies in Seattle," the cashier told her. "No one could predict something like this would happen."

Avery agreed. She paid for the popcorn and nearly bumped into Harrison as she exited the area.

"We're in luck," he said, proudly holding up a bag of Skittles.

"The only thing left in the cafeteria besides coffee was popcorn," she said, taking a handful from the top and sampling the salty goodness. Hungry as she was, it tasted like a slice of heaven.

"Shall we share our treats?" Harrison suggested.

"Ah . . ." Avery hesitated, not because she was unwilling to share, though.

"It makes sense, don't you think?" he quickly added. "If we're going to talk and get to know each other, we should at least be sitting together. Being close means we can pool our resources."

His reasoning made sense. She glanced over to where Beth and Olivia were and saw the woman with the tin box on one side and Beth and Olivia on the other side of her empty seat.

Harrison's gaze followed hers. "There's plenty of room where I'm at," he offered.

"I see," she reluctantly agreed.

Her lack of enthusiasm didn't appear to dampen his spirits, she noted.

"All right," she said. "I'll join you."

"Great." His smile was so big she feared his cheeks must ache.

Avery wondered if she was being led into a situation she would later regret. Impulsively, she'd agreed to his idea, and already she was having second thoughts. Rick had also had a lot of charm, had always been eager to spend time with her, too. But that hadn't stopped him from breaking her heart. Still, Harrison seemed sincere, and what could a short conversation hurt while they shared their snacks?

"I'll need to collect my overnight bag."

"I'll get it for you," he offered quickly, as if he feared she'd change her mind.

"It's okay. Let me explain what I'm doing to my two new friends." She handed Harrison the popcorn and went to retrieve the items she'd left behind.

"We saved your space," Olivia said, hopping down from where Avery had previously been sitting.

"Thank you. I met a new friend, and he asked me to sit with him," she explained as she reached for her rolling carry-on.

The middle-aged woman who sat to her left glanced up. "We can keep your seat in case you want to return," she said. "I'm Virginia," she added. "Do be careful, those sailors can be real charmers."

She appeared to have the same caution that Avery's grandmother had given her regarding men in the Navy.

"Thank you, Virginia. My name is Avery."

"Are you leaving?" Olivia wanted to know.

"Not really. I'm just sharing my popcorn with that man over there."

Olivia leaned forward as though to get a better look. She smiled, exposing her two missing front teeth. "He's cute."

"Is he?" Avery asked, pretending she hadn't noticed.

"Will you come back once you eat your popcorn?" Olivia asked. Her short legs swung back and forth anxiously.

"Would you like me to?"

"Yes, please. I like you and so does my mommy."

"Then I'll keep my bag right here," Avery said, pleased to have an excuse to return if she felt it was necessary. Why had she been so willing to give up her seat? Virginia was right. She needed to be wary.

When she joined Harrison, she heard the tail end of his conversation with his friends, which was basically telling them to back off. Avery was with him, and he wasn't willing to share her company. She pretended not to have heard, but her defenses went up like a border wall.

"I brought napkins," Avery said, breaking into the conversation.

Harrison greeted her with a warm welcome and an introduction. "This disreputable pair are my shipmates Dan and Kyle," he said, and motioned to the two other men.

"I'm pleased to meet you both."

"Likewise," the one named Kyle responded with a huge smile.

Harrison glared back at him and Kyle's grin instantly vanished.

Taking two napkins, she and Harrison divided the popcorn and Skittles evenly.

"What about your friends?" Avery asked, feeling guilty to be eating in front of them.

"I had a late breakfast," Dan explained, brushing off the offer.

"And I ate on base, so no worries," Kyle added. "You two go ahead and enjoy."

"I believe Kyle and Dan decided to take a stroll around the deck, isn't that right?" Harrison said, looking pointedly at his friends.

"Right," Kyle said, and Dan nodded.

"They can stay," Avery said quickly, smiling at the two other men. There was safety in numbers.

"No, they can't," Harrison countered like a lightning bolt had flashed into the room.

A Ferry Merry Christmas 53

"Right," Dan said. "Kyle and I need to make ourselves scarce."

The look Harrison gave his shipmates could have burned through steel.

After the two men wandered off, Avery glared at Harrison. "It wasn't necessary to make them leave, you know."

"I disagree," he countered. "I wanted the chance to talk to you without Kyle and Dan constantly butting in. Maybe it is selfish of me, but I only have this one chance to get to know you. I'm not about to squander that opportunity."

Avery appreciated Harrison's honesty and that he'd been up-front about his intentions.

"So," he said, "I'm guessing you live in the Bremerton area?"

"I do. I'm an accountant."

Harrison's thoughtful expression seemed to indicate he was absorbing the information. After a moment, he spoke. "That tells me that you're someone who's detailed, disciplined, and responsible."

How he was able to sum up her strongest qualities so quickly gave her pause. "I am. I like routine and work long hours, especially during tax season.

"Okay, my turn. Tell me about you?"

He shrugged as if to suggest he wasn't that interesting. Nevertheless, he said, "I joined the Navy out of high school and went to submarine school before being assigned to the base in Bangor, Maine."

"You mean to say there are two Bangor submarine bases? One on the East Coast and one on the West Coast? Guess that's to confuse the enemy, right?"

"I don't think that was the intention, but it could have been."

"Tell me more," she said, waving at him to continue.

"I've been in the Navy ten years and decided after my first tour of duty to make it my career." He said this as if he wasn't sure what to expect from her at this news.

Avery accepted then and there that this was not a relationship that would work for her. She saw no harm in continuing the conversation, in part because she believed in keeping her word. But as far as she was concerned, once the ferry reached Seattle, it was unlikely that she'd see Harrison again.

He watched her expectantly, as if wanting her to comment.

Avery said, "Sounds like you enjoy your job."

He nodded. "I do. In some ways I feel like I was *born* for this. I work with the missile defense system. I don't take that responsibility lightly."

She could appreciate his sense of duty, knowing he held life and death in his hands. "And you're patriotic."

Again, he agreed. "I love our country and am proud to serve it."

"And loyal to boot."

He chuckled. "That's me in a nutshell." He reached for a handful of popcorn mixed with the Skittles. "I confess I was pretty rebellious as a teenager, which is what prompted me, with a bit of encouragement from my parents, to enlist. Dad felt the discipline would do me some good and he was right. It didn't take beyond the first day of boot camp to understand my life was about to change drastically."

The more they talked, the more Avery found herself liking Harrison, which was unfortunate. If he had a regular job and lived nearby, she might even be tempted to agree to go on a date with him. But as things stood, this conversation would be the extent of their involvement.

Dan and Kyle returned from their stroll around the deck.

"Is it safe for us to return?" Kyle asked, sending Harrison a teasing look.

Dan was on the phone. From the bits of conversation Avery heard, it appeared he was talking to his wife and explaining the situation.

"I don't have any idea how long this will take," he said. "None of us do."

Avery checked the time. An hour had passed and there had yet to be an update. A lot of the passengers were getting restless, moving about, complaining to one another. The room reverberated with discontent.

Dan ended his call. "The wife is worried I'm going to miss the family party. And I obviously can't promise her I'll be there until we get some word as to what's the problem."

"Everyone is wondering. It's already been an hour," Avery said, looking around the room. She'd been too wrapped up in her conversation with Harrison to pay much attention. The grumbling seemed to get louder by the minute as the passengers grew impatient.

The squeaky sound came from the loudspeaker, indicating another announcement was imminent. The murmurs waned as everyone prepared to listen.

"This is your captain again. I'm afraid I have some unfortunate news."

Avery heard several curses and loud complaints followed by shushing from other passengers as the captain continued.

"It's been determined that the engine problem can't be resolved quickly. We need a part, which fortunately is available. The replacement part will be delivered as quickly as possible. That's the bad news. The good news is that the fix will take a relatively short amount of time once the part is here. I appreciate your patience."

"Oh dear," Avery murmured. She hated the thought of her brother waiting around the Seattle ferry terminal for hours on end. It was clear she wouldn't make the lunch reservation.

"I know a lot of you are anxious, wondering how long we are expected to wait," Captain Douglas continued. "I don't have a definitive answer, I'm sorry to say. Again, I ask for your patience."

As soon as the announcement was over, myriad angry voices filled the room until the cacophony made it difficult to hear, let alone think. People were upset. Avery understood; she was disappointed herself. This wasn't how she'd planned her Christmas holiday to start. It was hard enough to keep her spirits high, missing her grandmother as much as she did. Now this.

Caught up in her own frustration, she barely noticed the man in the seat across from where she sat. Earlier, she'd picked him out as a businessman or maybe a lawyer, by the looks of his briefcase.

"This can't be happening," he lamented loudly. "Not now. Please, not now."

Most everyone ignored him. Avery couldn't. Something was happening that was causing him great distress and it was more than being late for a family gathering or disappointing his wife.

"Is everything all right?" she asked, leaning forward enough to touch his arm.

"No." The man sat up, then rammed his fingers through his hair. "This is a disaster."

"Is there anything I can do to help?" she asked.

He shook his head so hard she feared his glasses would fly across the room. "No, there's nothing anyone can do. My wife is pregnant and went into labor this morning. We moved to Seattle this summer for my job and don't have any family here. She's all alone."

Listening in on the conversation, Harrison gave a low whistle, and the two men introduced themselves. The man's name was James.

"The baby isn't due for another two weeks," James continued. "Lilly's had a difficult pregnancy and needs me with her. She's frantic and I'm stuck on this blasted ferry."

"My buddy is a medic," Harrison said. "Let me get him. He might be able to help."

"How?" James asked, looking up hopefully.

Harrison collected Dan, who sat down next to James. "You said your wife is in labor?"

James nodded. "She isn't completely sure—at least

she wasn't when we first left Bremerton. Now she said the pains are continuing, so she's thinking this might be it."

"And she's alone?"

James nodded again.

"Is there someone close by who can come sit with her until you arrive? That will help with the anxiety she's feeling."

"But I need to be there," James insisted.

"And you soon will be," Dan assured him.

Avery added her opinion. "This should all be resolved in no time, and we'll be on our way."

James frowned, doubt showing in his eyes.

"I don't know much about the birthing process," Dan admitted. "My wife gave birth while I was at sea. What I do know is that the first baby generally doesn't come quickly. It will be hours before your wife is ready to deliver."

"Hours," James repeated, and sighed with relief.

Avery certainly hoped that would be the case for James and Lilly.

CHAPTER FIVE

"Mommy, does Daddy know the ferryboat is stuck?" Olivia asked.

Beth Sullivan placed her arm around her daughter's small shoulders and rested her chin on top of Olivia's head. "Probably not, sweetie." She wasn't sure about anything these days. Her life was in turmoil, her future uncertain.

Her husband had left her and Olivia two years ago. Two lonely, tortuous years. Yet not a day passed when Olivia didn't bring up her father. Beth simply didn't know how best to explain that Logan had decided he no longer wanted to be married. His discontent started when he learned Beth's parents had helped with the medical expenses following Olivia's birth. Born at thirty-five weeks, a full seven weeks before she was due, problems had developed with Olivia's lungs. Weighing barely five pounds, their infant daughter had been placed in the NICU for three days. Their health insurance covered only part of the hospital fees. The bills compounded further as they became a one-income family.

Logan grew depressed and withdrawn, as if the financial help had somehow made him even less of a man. Gone were the evenings when they'd snuggled in front of the television or when they'd talked late into the night. Beth didn't know what to do. It felt like she'd married a stranger.

A month after he discovered the truth, with little more than some weak excuse, Logan moved out and suggested she file for a divorce.

The pregnancy with Olivia hadn't been planned. Beth had been on birth control and they weren't financially ready to start a family. The morning sickness had been terrible the first few months. She hadn't been able to hold down anything for weeks. But Logan had been wonderful. He'd stood with her and held her hair back as she threw up her breakfast morning after morning. When the doctor prescribed a drug that was safe for her to take that would help ease her discomfort, he'd blanched at the cost. Beth had, too, and that was only the beginning. Soon the medical bills seemed astronomical.

After the first three months, Beth was back to normal. While the pregnancy had been a surprise, Beth was happy and glowing. Logan went with her to every doctor appointment. They both loved their baby long before Olivia was born.

Their tight finances became even tighter, only getting worse as the full weight of paying the bills fell solely on her husband.

She noticed that Logan rarely laughed anymore and became obsessed over the mounting bills. Working as a carpenter, he was often out of work for short stretches of time, which led to them going deeper and deeper into debt. Around the time Olivia turned two, her mother noticed how stressed out Beth was. When she learned the degree to which the young couple continued to struggle making even the minimum payments for the crippling medical bills, her parents had stepped in to help. Knowing how proud Logan was, Beth didn't tell him. But it didn't take her husband long to notice, and once he did, everything changed.

Beth tried to make amends, but nothing she said or did seemed to make a difference. She cooked his favorite dinner only to watch him stir the food around on his plate. Their healthy love life went down the drain until they did nothing more than sleep in the same bed. Whatever troubled Logan, Beth believed, was more than the assistance her parents had given them. She thought it might have something to do with his work. Again and again she tried to get Logan to talk to her, but every effort was met with denials.

It was like he gave up on their marriage and, sadly, on himself. Little she said or did could bring him out of his depression. Sick at heart, Beth felt that she had let him down by accepting her parents' help.

She offered to return to work, even though she preferred to be a full-time mom. Logan was against it, claiming daycare costs were prohibitive and it didn't make sense for her to work and then pay nearly every cent she earned to the childcare center. Besides, he also wanted Beth to be at home with Olivia, as no one would love and care for her better than her mother would. The situation continued unresolved for two full years as they both struggled to keep their heads above water financially while their marriage limped along. Then a bout of unemployment became the final straw.

When Logan moved out, it had devastated Beth. No matter how hard she tried to convince him to stay, his mind was set. He decided to live elsewhere, packed his bags, and was gone.

Olivia loved her father and missed him terribly. It

broke Beth's heart to have her daughter ask when her daddy would come back. Even now, two years after he'd moved out, the six-year-old talked about her father constantly.

Beth didn't know how she would have survived without her parents' help. They paid the rent on her small apartment because her income as a substitute teacher wasn't enough to meet her financial obligations, even with the money Logan gave her each month. With Olivia entering first grade the next school year, Beth planned to return to work full-time.

Logan faithfully paid child support and came for Olivia every other weekend, spending Saturday with their daughter. Because he was renting a room in a friend's house, he couldn't keep her overnight. They rarely spoke, and if they did, Logan's first question was to inquire if she'd seen an attorney yet. He seemed eager to end their marriage. Beth hoped that in time Logan would realize how much she loved him, that he would miss them both enough that he would come home. More than anything, she longed for their marriage to survive.

Olivia leaned against her arm, breaking into her thoughts.

"I'm not going to be able to see Santa, am I?" Olivia said, sighing, as the reality of their situation hit home.

"We don't know that yet," Beth said, trying to sound optimistic. It didn't look promising, though. The information on visiting Santa stated that he was only available until 3:00. The captain's last announcement was discouraging. Beth couldn't imagine that this was a quick fix, seeing that a part had to be found and delivered, and then the engine repaired. It went without saying that this delay could last for hours. By the time they docked, Santa was sure to be heading back to the North Pole.

Thinking it might be best to prepare Olivia for the disappointment, she asked, "If we can't see Santa, will that make you sad?"

Olivia twisted her head to one side as she considered her answer.

After a few minutes of thinking matters through, she said, "If Santa needs to get home before the ferryboat is fixed, I'll understand."

"That's a great attitude." Beth was proud of how well her daughter had taken the frustrating news.

"It's what Miss Avery said that convinced me. Not every little girl and boy gets to talk to Santa to tell him their Christmas wishes. That means if I don't see him today, that'll be okay, because he already knows what I really want for Christmas."

"That's true, sweetheart. Thank you for being so patient," Beth commented, but her daughter wasn't listening.

"Mommy," Olivia said excitedly, grabbing hold of Beth's arm. "Is that Daddy over there?" Olivia quickly slid off the chair and raced over to a tall man in a black leather jacket.

The blood rushed from Beth's face. It was her husband. He must have recently climbed the stairwell up from the car deck.

With her arms open wide, Olivia ran up to Logan. "Daddy, Daddy, you're here."

At the sound of Olivia's voice, he whirled around. He looked as shocked as Beth was.

"Pumpkin, what are you doing here?"

Breathless with excitement, Oliva spoke in a rush. "Mommy is taking me to see Santa, but he might be gone by the time we get to Seattle. I told her it was all right. Santa's got me covered."

Logan looked to where Beth was sitting, and their eyes met and held. It'd been two months or longer since they'd exchanged more than a few words. On his weekends, he collected Olivia and dropped her off and that was it. She often stood in the open doorway as he drove away with their daughter, her heart aching.

Beth watched Olivia follow Logan into the cafeteria, where he purchased a cup of coffee.

Grabbing hold of Logan's sleeve, Olivia pulled him over to where they'd been sitting.

Logan reluctantly followed Olivia back to where Beth waited.

"You can have my seat," Olivia said, her face bright with joy at seeing her father.

Beth knew this was awkward for them both. For Olivia's sake, she pretended running into her soon-to-be ex-husband was no big deal.

Logan sat where Olivia had indicated, next to Beth.

"Merry Christmas, Logan," Beth said.

He nodded and stared at his coffee as if he was reading tea leaves.

After a couple uneasy moments, he asked, "Are you and Olivia doing okay?"

"We're great," she said cheerfully, although she doubted she'd fooled him. "What about you?"

Logan shrugged. "I got laid off in October . . . construction work, well, you know. On again, off again. I went back last week, and thankfully it's a long-term project."

That he'd continued paying support even when he wasn't working must have been a hardship. Beth appreciated that he hadn't forgotten or abandoned his obligation toward Olivia. No matter how difficult financially, he'd been faithful with child support.

"Did you know I lost both my front teeth?" Olivia asked. She stood in front of her father with a huge grin, displaying the large gap between her teeth.

"You told me on the phone," Logan reminded her. In a whisper he added for Beth's ears, "About a hundred times."

"Did I tell you the Tooth Fairy brought me a dollar for each tooth?" Olivia asked.

"You did."

"Sarah at school got five dollars when she lost a tooth. Can you imagine a whole five dollars? I'd start pulling all my teeth if I got five dollars for every tooth."

Logan laughed, and because he did, Beth smiled.

"Are you spending Christmas with your parents?" he asked Beth.

She nodded. "What are your Christmas plans?" He'd been raised in California and didn't have much of a family. He rarely mentioned anything having to do with his childhood, and when she asked, he often changed the subject.

He shrugged, indicating he didn't have any plans.

"You should come and be with us for Christmas," Olivia piped in with enthusiasm that was hard to ignore. "It would be the best Christmas ever if you came to Grandma and Grandpa's with us."

"I . . . I don't think so, pumpkin. Your grandparents—"

"They aren't mad at you," Olivia said, cutting him off. "Grandpa told me that sometimes daddies need time away to think things over and that you would always love me no matter what, but I get sad when you aren't here."

At her words, Logan swallowed tightly.

Beth had no idea her father had spoken to Olivia about Logan's absence from their lives.

"He said that, did he?" Logan sounded doubtful.

Olivia's head bobbed up and down. "He really did. So will you come for Christmas? It would be the best gift ever if you did."

After a brief hesitation, Logan said, "I'll think about it."

Olivia released a loud sigh as her shoulders sank. "That's what Mommy says all the time, and it almost always means no."

Once more Logan smiled and looked at Beth. "My parents said the same thing to me, and Olivia's right, it nearly always meant no."

Olivia pleaded, folding her hands as if praying. "It would make me so happy if you were with us for Christmas."

"Pumpkin . . ."

Olivia wasn't hearing it. "Grandma makes the best

stuffing in the entire world, and she puts it right inside the turkey and everything just like Thanksgiving. And there's mashed potatoes and lots of gravy with cranberry sauce. I don't like that much, but I take one bite. Mommy calls it a thank-you bite, which means I'm grateful enough to give it a try."

Breathless by the time she finished, Olivia looked pleadingly at her father. "Will you please, please, please come for Christmas?"

Logan seemed to take in his daughter's words. "You say you're sad without me, but is your mommy sad, too?" Although he asked Olivia the question, it was directed at Beth.

"It's okay," Beth quickly responded, not allowing Olivia to answer. "Olivia and I have learned to adjust."

Olivia twisted her head as though to study her father. "Are you sad without us, too?"

Again, he responded with a shrug as if he wasn't sure what to say. "Sometimes, but like your mother said, I've adjusted."

Olivia mulled this over. "Is it possible for adults to get unadjusted?"

Logan shared a surprised look with Beth. "I don't know."

"Neither do I," Beth added.

They sat in silence for several seconds.

"I had no idea you were on the ferry," Beth commented, wanting to fill in the uncomfortable pause.

"Yeah, I'm selling my motorcycle."

Beth swallowed hard, knowing how much Logan loved his Harley. He'd earned money washing cars at a dealership as a teenager until he'd saved up enough to pay for the bike. He treasured it more than any other possession he owned.

"No, you can't," she said, without realizing she'd spoken aloud. The money situation would have to be dire if Logan had resorted to selling his beloved motorcycle.

"It is what it is," Logan murmured.

"I remember your motorcycle!" Olivia cried excitedly. "You promised to give me a ride one day. Remember?"

"I do, and perhaps I'll buy another one someday. I always keep my promises, Olivia. You'll get your ride, I guarantee it, I'm just not sure when."

"But I like the motorcycle you have now."

"So do I," Logan said, sadness leaking into his response.

"Then why are you selling it?" Olivia asked, which was the very question plaguing Beth.

Logan appeared to be composing his answer. "Sometimes adults have to give up things they enjoy for other things."

"What other things?" Olivia asked.

"Just things, ones that are important."

Beth battled back tears. It hurt her heart that Logan was selling his motorcycle. As hard as it was to make ends meet, especially when she wasn't working, not once had they considered selling his bike.

Reaching over, Beth placed her hand on Logan's forearm. "I'm so sorry."

He looked at her hand for several long seconds. "Nothing to be sorry about. Like I said, it is what it is. Life is like that. We all need to make choices, and they aren't always easy ones. I've got my truck, and the motorcycle was taking up space and . . ." He let the rest fade.

"Your truck is twenty years old," she protested. It had been on its last legs when they'd been together. She couldn't imagine it would keep running much longer.

"It gets me where I need to go and that's all that's necessary."

Beth hardly knew what to say.

"Mommy, please call Grandma and tell her Daddy is coming to dinner on Christmas."

Beth knew Olivia's real Christmas wish was to spend it with her father—spend it as a family. For that matter, it would mean the world to her, too. The last two Christmases without him had left her feeling empty and her heart aching for what might have been.

"Would you like that?" she asked Logan, unsure of his response.

He turned to look at her, his gaze intense. "Would you?"

"I would," and then for emphasis, she nodded. "More than you know."

His eyes filled with a flicker of what looked like hope. "You can ask, but I don't think your folks would relish me hanging around."

"I will ask, but I feel that despite everything, they would welcome you," she told him. Her parents knew how much it would mean to Olivia to have her father over for Christmas and would relent if for no other reason.

He remained uncertain. "You're sure. I mean, even after, you know . . . everything?"

"Olivia is right. Mom and Dad would be happy to see you."

"Then okay, if you're sure," he said.

Beth reached for her phone. It was a small step, and for the first time in a long while it was a step forward.

CHAPTER SIX

Kellie Stetler glanced at her phone for the second time in the last five minutes, awaiting an update from her brother, Harrison. He said he was lucky enough to catch the 11:45 ferry out of Bremerton. *Lucky* wasn't the word she would use currently. The ferry sat dead in the water in the middle of Puget Sound halfway between Bremerton and Seattle.

Having lived and worked in the Seattle area for several years, Kellie had never heard of anything like this happening to a ferry. This was highly unusual, and its being this close to Christmas made it even more frustrating.

Harrison hadn't sent any updates beyond a couple short text messages, giving her the most current information, which, to be honest, wasn't much. It didn't take a mind reader to know his fellow passengers wouldn't be pleased with this unexpected turn of events. She could only imagine how upset everyone on board must be. Everyone had a reason to get to Seattle, and if the traffic in the ferry terminal was any indication, there were plenty of friends and family awaiting the boat's arrival.

The lone announcement at the Seattle terminal was less than helpful. All Kellie had heard was that the Bremerton run had been delayed. The crowd inside the building was growing by the minute. First with people waiting for the ferry's arrival, in addition to the ticket holders expecting to board for the return trip.

"Excuse me," a man said, coming to stand next to Kellie.

Kellie glanced up from her phone. She'd noticed him earlier, as he'd looked familiar.

"I promise this isn't a pickup line, but I know I've seen you somewhere before." He wore a slight frown, as though racking his brain to make the connection.

Kellie placed her phone inside her purse. "To be honest, I was thinking the same thing . . . that we'd previously met." He was attractive enough for her to remember, tall and fit, with brown hair and eyes the color of rich, dark chocolate. His face was familiar, but she couldn't imagine where they might have met.

"I'm Reed Bond. Does that name ring a bell?"

She repeated it inside her head. "No. I'm Kellie Stetler."

After a moment he shook his head.

Because she spent a great deal of her time at work, she wondered if that was the connection. "I work for Microsoft."

Reed snapped his fingers. "I do, too. I attended a workshop you ran a year or so back on product development. It blew me away."

"Yes, yes," she said, now remembering him as well. In a room full of employees, she recalled his intelligent questions and the insight he offered after her presentation. In fact, she'd taken one of his ideas back to the development department and it had since been implemented. She'd tried to thank him personally, only to discover he was away from the office, traveling for the company. She'd made sure he was given the credit but had hoped to contact him directly. Eventually reaching out to him had slipped her mind. Their meeting had taken place shortly after her breakup with Jude, at a time when she was struggling emotionally.

"It's good to see you again," Reed said. "I take it you're waiting for someone on the Bremerton ferry?"

"My brother."

"I'm waiting for my sister; she lives and works in Bremerton as a CPA."

"Harrison's a submariner. I haven't seen him in a couple years. I hope whatever the problem is, it can be easily handled. This will be our first Christmas together in a long time."

"My sister is coming to spend Christmas with me, too. I've never known anything like this to happen with the ferries before, have you?"

"Never," she agreed.

"I was thinking," Reed said, and shifted his weight from one foot to the other as though uneasy. "I made a lunch reservation for me and Avery at her favorite seafood restaurant. Clearly, she isn't going to be able to make it. Would you care to have lunch with me?"

Kellie had made it a hard-and-fast rule not to get involved with anyone at work, so she hesitated. Then she abruptly decided why not, it was the holiday season, and it was just lunch. Besides, reservations this time of year were hard to get. It seemed a shame to waste it.

"Sure," she said. "That certainly beats standing around here, waiting for information."

"Anthony's is within walking distance, so if we see the ferry is docking, we can hightail it back in time to meet your brother and my sister."

"That sounds like a plan," Kellie agreed.

Reed grinned. "The reservation was for an hour ago,

but fortunately I was able to adjust the time, as there'd been a cancellation at the last minute."

They left the terminal and Kellie looked up at the silver clouds that darkened the sky. "It feels like it's cold enough to snow," she commented.

"I didn't hear that snow was predicted. Weather, like holiday plans, has a way of changing without notice."

"True," Kellie agreed.

As they walked side by side, Kellie's foot slipped on a patch of ice. She would have taken a tumble if Reed hadn't caught her arm and held her upright. "Oh my," she said, her heart pumping. This was her fault. She should have been watching where she stepped. Instead, she'd been distracted with the thoughts of Jude. He certainly wasn't thinking about her. Within a week of their parting, Jude was in another relationship, which left her to speculate how long the two had been seeing each other behind her back.

After Jude, Kellie had gotten gun-shy and had buried herself in work, unwilling to trust her own judgment when it came to men and relationships. She'd been so sure, confident she and Jude would spend their lives together.

"Thank you," she whispered, clinging to his arm.

"My pleasure. I can't have my lunch date getting hurt on our way to the restaurant."

As they neared Anthony's, the sidewalks came alive with people dashing in and out of the popular stores along the tourist-rich waterfront. The scents of Christmas were everywhere. A vendor sold spiced hot apple cider on the street. Evergreens decorated the open seating areas that dotted the small fish-and-chips stands along the way. Their aroma wafted toward them as Kellie and Reed walked past.

"I do so love Christmas," Kellie commented. "There's such an air of happy anticipation." A little girl walked past, holding the hand of her father and licking a candy cane.

"I love Christmas, too," Reed said.

"And I'm so happy that I'm able to spend it with my brother. He's been a real trooper over the last year, texting and emailing me uplifting messages. He made it a point to find something to make me smile." Kellie didn't realize what she'd said until the words escaped her mouth.

"It's been a rough year?" Reed asked.

She didn't want to go down this uncomfortable path, so she blew it off. "No more than usual, I guess. You know, life in general." Her thoughts drifted, unbidden, to Jude again. She'd been convinced he was the one. The summer before their breakup, Jude had met her parents. She'd assumed the weekend had gone well. Not until after they'd split did her mother mention she was relieved they'd parted. From the moment she'd met Jude, her mom felt he wasn't the right man for Kellie. In retrospect, Kellie wished her mother had said something then, although she had to wonder if she would have listened.

"I see." It was apparent Reed had read through her words and knew it was much more. She was grateful he didn't press for details.

They reached Anthony's and Reed announced his name to the hostess.

"I'm pleased you were able to make it," the young woman said. "In another five minutes we would have had to release the reservation."

"I'm glad we made it, too," Reed told her.

"Weren't you the one who was waiting for the Bremerton ferry?" the pretty young woman asked.

"Yes, I called earlier."

"I thought so. That stalled ferry is big news. Everyone is talking about it. I can't remember anything like this happening before, and right before Christmas, too."

"For sure the timing is bad, but I doubt anyone wants to be trapped on a ferry any time of the year."

The hostess agreed and led them to a table by the window. "I saved this table for you so you can keep watch in case the ferry docks."

"That was thoughtful," Kellie said, appreciating the kind gesture.

They sat and opened their menus. A server appeared and took their drink order. Needing something to chase away the chill from the short walk, Kellie asked for a hot buttered rum. Reed ordered the same.

The drinks were promptly delivered, and they delayed placing their meal order, wanting to enjoy them. The hot alcoholic beverage instantly went to Kellie's head. She should have known better than to drink it on an empty stomach. Brushing her shoulder-length auburn hair around her ear, she took in a deep, brain-clearing breath.

"Thank you. This is a lovely respite from waiting in the ferry terminal."

"My pleasure." Reed relaxed against the back of his cushioned chair.

The server delivered warm sourdough bread with herb butter to the table. They both took a slice.

Not wanting to talk about herself, Kellie said, "Tell me about your sister."

Reed's eyes sparkled with affection. "Avery is the best. We were raised by our grandparents. Gramps died

A Ferry Merry Christmas 83

my first year of college and Avery stayed with our grandmother until she graduated from college. Grams wanted her to have a life of her own, so Avery rented a cozy apartment until it became apparent Grandma's health was steadily declining. My sister moved back home and cared for her until her death. As far as I'm concerned, Avery is a saint."

He took a breath and waited until she waved him on, wanting him to continue.

"I did what I could to help. Unfortunately, I travel a lot for work, and so my sister handled the brunt of the caregiving. As a result, she's twenty-five and doesn't have much of a social life.

"I tried introducing her to a few of my friends. Big mistake. In fact, I'd arranged for a friend to join us here today. As soon as she heard of my latest matchmaking attempt, she point-blank refused."

"I was thinking I would introduce my brother to a couple of women from the office. Guessing it won't be appreciated if he feels the way Avery does."

"What about you?" Reed asked, holding her gaze. "Are you currently involved with someone?"

"No. Are you?"

"No," he said, as if this was exactly what he wanted to hear and hoped she felt the same.

Although skeptical that this would lead to more

than a pleasant lunch, Kellie smiled, pleased that their mutual single status was established.

Grinning, Reed briefly glanced down at his drink before making eye contact. "I have a confession. You should know, I recognized you right away. I debated awhile about how best to approach you and decided to pretend. I admired you the first time we met at that presentation and considered asking you out."

"Why didn't you?"

He looked away. "With all the traveling I do, it's hard to maintain a relationship. And I figured you were probably already involved. I have a sense that you were?" His words were more a question than a statement.

For a moment, Kellie was too surprised to answer.

He took her silence to mean something else.

"I apologize, I shouldn't have asked you that."

"Actually," she said, "at the time we first met, I was seeing someone else. Someone in my department." She sipped her drink. "I learned my lesson and have decided against dating men who work for Microsoft."

"Even in a different department?" he pressed.

"Well . . . no. I think if I were to meet someone from a department that doesn't work closely with mine, then it could possibly work."

Reed's grin was huge. "Great."

"What about you? I mean, at the time we first met?" she asked.

"No one. Like I mentioned, I work long hours that take me out of town far more than is healthy for a long-term relationship. I had my twenty-eighth birthday a while back and it sort of hit me then that I needed to be thinking about the goals I have for the future." He paused and looked away as though embarrassed. "I apologize. I didn't mean for this conversation to go in that direction. We've only just met, and I doubt you want to hear about my life goals at our first lunch."

Kellie relaxed. "It's not a problem. I'm one of those people who appreciate honesty." Especially someone who makes it known he isn't one to lead a woman on for his own selfish reasons.

Again, her thoughts drifted back to Jude. She'd believed he had the same goals as she did—marriage, children, and a future together. After three years it seemed like it was time to move forward, only for Kellie to discover Jude had no intention of marrying her. How foolish she felt to have wasted those years on a man who'd misled and used her.

In retrospect, she realized Jude had manipulated her to get the promotion he wanted. She'd foolishly assumed that once he had advanced in his career to the point that they were equals in the workplace they would marry. Not so, she learned shortly after he got what he'd wanted. It was then that Kellie was forced to face the truth.

Thankfully, they'd never moved in together, so they were both able to go on with their lives with minimal fuss. Which is exactly what Jude had done.

The server collected their orders. Kellie went with the Cajun spiced rockfish and Reed ordered the coconut shrimp with a Caesar salad. They enjoyed their meal in a companionable silence.

"I wonder if there is any news," Kellie said as she reached for her phone to check if Harrison had sent a text with an update.

"Anything?" Reed asked while she scrolled through her notifications.

Kellie nodded. "Not from my brother. However, from what's being reported in the news, it's an engine problem. Supposedly, it could be a simple fix once they can get the part to the ferry."

"You mean the part has to be found and then delivered?"

"It looks that way," Kellie murmured.

"Then it could take several more hours."

Again, she agreed. "Unfortunately." Looking up, she was surprised to find Reed smiling.

A Ferry Merry Christmas

"Do you have plans for the rest of the day?" he asked.

Under normal circumstances, she'd head back to her condo in Kirkland and wait for Harrison to catch an Uber. That had been the original plan. These, however, weren't normal circumstances.

"What do you have in mind?" she asked.

"Have you ever taken a ride on Seattle's Great Wheel?"

She shook her head. "No, but I've always wanted to someday."

"Well, it looks like someday has arrived. We should be able to see the ferry from the top. You game?"

Kellie was intrigued. This sounded like a great way to kill time. "You bet."

"Great. Let's go."

Kellie grabbed her coat, which she'd rested over the back of the empty chair next to her, and stood. What had looked to be a long, miserable afternoon waiting for her brother had suddenly turned into what might be a grand adventure.

CHAPTER SEVEN

Even with her defenses up, Avery found Harrison entertaining, easy to talk to, both amusing and intelligent. She liked that he didn't seem to mind the wait, showing patience and a positive attitude. Certainly, chatting with him helped the time pass. Otherwise, Avery would have been bored and restless like many of her fellow passengers.

"I found the best way to get to know someone is to ask questions," he said, holding the last of the popcorn in his hand.

"That works for me so long as it's a two-way street."

He gestured toward her. "Ask away. My life is an open book."

She eyed him carefully. "Okay, tell me about your last serious relationship and why you split."

He groaned. "Sorry, I'm not willing to walk through that minefield."

Avery couldn't help it, she laughed.

His brow creased with speculation. "You did that on purpose, didn't you? What was that—some kind of test?"

"You passed," she said, still having trouble holding back her amusement.

"I suppose you're going to bring up religion next."

"No, you're off the hook."

"Good. My turn."

She nodded and signaled for him to continue. "Have at it."

"All right," he said, as if thinking hard. "Tell me your favorite childhood memory."

She mulled over her answer. "That's deep. Let me think." There'd been several that immediately came to mind. One, however, stood out. "I was around eight or nine and wanted more than anything to visit Disneyland. As young as I was, I knew a trip that expensive was more than my grandparents could afford. Instead, we drove to South Dakota, where my great-grandparents once had a farm. We saw Mount Rushmore and met all kinds of relatives. One of my great-uncles still farmed wheat. I ate corn right off the cob and got to hold piglets and milk a cow. It was amazing." Reliving those memories warmed her heart.

They continued with the questions, each taking a turn. Harrison was right, this was a good way to learn about each other and what was important.

Although they were involved in their discussion, Avery couldn't help noticing that those milling around the area were growing increasingly impatient at the time it was taking to get the ferry up and running again. Crew members came and went but offered little in the way of information. Voices were getting louder as people grew more and more agitated.

"Hey, look." The middle-aged man with the glasses who was part of the band sat in one of the booths. Excitedly, he pointed out the window. Several commuters raced to the side of the ferry. The musician stood, directing others to what he was staring at in the distance.

Harrison moved closer to the window to get a better view.

"What is it?" Avery asked, curious herself.

"It's another ferry," he told her, wearing a puzzled frown.

"It's empty," the band guy shouted, then added for emphasis, "The ferry is completely empty. No cars. No passengers. That ferry should be coming to rescue us.

Instead, it's sailing directly past us and heading to Seattle while we're trapped here."

"Empty?" Avery repeated, wondering what that might mean.

As if reading her mind, Harrison suggested, "I imagine the Department of Transportation is sending another ferry to Seattle to replace this one."

"It certainly looks that way," James agreed. Avery had glanced his way every now and again. The poor guy, who sat with his shoulders slumped forward, kept an anxious study of his phone, as if he expected it to ring at any moment. He'd mentioned that a neighbor had come to sit with his wife and that helped relieve his mind somewhat. It couldn't be easy to see an empty ferry pass him by, though.

It made sense that the WSDOT would look for a way to solve the problem by recruiting another ferry. With the *Yakima* breaking down, the backlog of passengers and cars waiting must have crowded the already busy streets of Seattle. The terminal must be bursting with walk-on traffic.

It was crewman Earl Jones's bad timing that he should walk through the passenger deck just as the other ferry sailed past.

"Hey," the band leader shouted, waylaying Earl. "There's an empty ferry out there."

Earl paused mid-step and turned to face the angry crowd. "Yeah, I know. The backup in Seattle is closing down streets and . . ."

"Why are you not more concerned about us, instead of what's happening in Seattle?" someone Avery couldn't see shouted. Whoever it was did nothing to disguise his anger.

"We'll be on our way soon enough," Earl said, as if placating a child.

"How soon?" James demanded. He rose to his feet and raised his hand in the air to gather Earl's attention. "I need to get to Seattle. I don't have time to waste sitting around here twiddling my thumbs while—"

He was cut off by a volley of irritated voices.

"My band is stuck here, too, you know," the guy by the window shouted. "We're supposed to be playing for a wedding."

"Hey, hey, people, settle down," Earl cried, his voice loud enough to garner attention. "I get it. No one is happy with the situation. Complaining isn't going to change anything. Just relax . . . The necessary part is sure to arrive anytime now."

"Relax? You want us to relax?" someone else said with a loud, disbelieving groan. "Are you kidding me right now?"

"You mean to say the part hasn't even arrived?"

A loud rumble of unhappy voices filled the area.

"We should sue the state." The suggestion came in the form of a shout.

"Yeah. Anyone here an attorney?" another person asked.

A bevy of loud discontentment rolled through the deck like a tsunami after an earthquake.

"We've already been here well over an hour," the grandmotherly woman with the tin box of cookies in her lap said. "How much longer is this going to take?"

Earl Jones held up his hands as if someone had pointed a gun at him. "Quiet down. Quiet down. You're all talking at once. I can't make sense out of anything you're saying."

His plea was ignored.

"You be quiet."

"Yeah. You're no help whatsoever."

"You have to wonder what kind of people the state hires to operate these ferries."

"Who is responsible for the maintenance of these ferries, anyway?"

"You're right, we should sue."

Looking completely exasperated, Earl demanded, "Sue us for what?"

"For emotional distress," a woman shouted. "I'm missing my family's celebration. It's the first one in five years. My grandmother flew all the way from New Jersey to be with us."

"I'm supposed to pick up my kids for Christmas," a man shouted. "I have no way of letting my ex know why I'm late, since she's blocked my number. She'll probably take me to court to keep my children away from me after this."

"I'm sorry, folks," Earl said. "I know everyone has places to go and people to see. It's an unfortunate set of circumstances."

"You think this is unfortunate?" a man standing in the back said with a groan. "I'll tell you what's unfortunate. I have tickets to see *The Nutcracker* with my daughter. I paid a small fortune for those tickets."

Another voice chimed in. "My boss said if I was late one more time, I should look for another job. I'm late because this ferry never seems to run on schedule. What's with you people, anyway?"

Earl eased his way to the stairwell. "I'm sorry, folks, but I can't tell you anything more. I'm just as eager to reach Seattle as you are."

"Yeah, right."

Having said his piece, Earl flew down the stairs as if escaping a burning building.

Avery didn't blame him. The longer he remained on the passenger deck, the louder the chaos became. She understood everyone's frustration. For her own part, it hadn't been as frustrating as it was for the others. Her only concern was her brother.

She hated the thought of Reed waiting at the ferry terminal. He'd texted earlier and assured her he was able to change their lunch reservation. That time had long since passed. Avery hoped he had the good sense to head back to his condo and wait for news. He lived within walking distance of the waterfront.

Considering the news that the repair part had yet to arrive, she needed to let him know this wait was going to be longer than anticipated.

Reaching for her phone, she started to text and then decided she'd rather talk to him personally.

He answered on the third ring, and she wondered if he hadn't been able to hear the call for all the activity and noise in the terminal.

"Hey, there. Any news?" he asked.

From the sounds of cars honking and Christmas music playing in the background, he must have decided to head home.

"Reed, I'm sorry you had to cancel the reservation. I should have called earlier to let you know I wasn't going to be able to make it."

"No problem." He didn't need to sound so cheerful about it. She'd been looking forward to their lunch.

"What's up?"

"Unfortunately, not much. It doesn't look promising that I'll arrive anytime soon."

"That's okay. Oh, and I kept the reservation."

"You did?" On the one hand she was pleased, and on the other she was disappointed that she hadn't been there to enjoy the seafood with him.

"Actually, the ferry breaking down worked out better than I could have expected." Once more he sounded like he was ready to do a happy dance that she was being held as a virtual prisoner on the dark waters of Puget Sound.

"It worked to your advantage, did it?" She wasn't sure how she felt about that.

"I ran into Kellie at the terminal," he went on to explain. "I'd briefly met her once before; we both work for Microsoft."

Ah, now she understood and was pleased for him.

"Seeing that you weren't going to make it, Kellie agreed to join me for lunch. We're just leaving Anthony's now."

Any lingering resentment she held immediately melted away. "That's great." It was nice to hear her brother sounding so relaxed and happy.

"It's good to know you aren't hanging around the terminal with nothing to do," Avery said. "I'll update you when I have some solid information."

"Great."

"No need to wait for me. I'll walk to your condo—"

Reed interrupted her before she could finish. "Kellie and I are headed to Pike Place Market. She's waiting for someone, too, so we decided to hang out together."

Avery smiled. Well, at least someone was benefiting from the delay. She ended the call and replaced her phone inside her purse. Dan and Kyle returned to the seats in one of the rows toward the back of the deck. Avery was certain Harrison had sent them on their way while she'd been on the phone. He seemed determined to win her over in the short time they had together.

"Everything okay with your brother?" Harrison asked.

"Better than I expected. He ran into a woman from work. He didn't say much, but it sounds like they're having a grand old time exploring the city."

"That's great."

Avery thought so, too. She glanced over at James and noticed that he continued to nervously study his phone.

"Any news from your wife?" she asked, leaning closer so he would be able to hear her.

He looked up and nodded. "Lilly's pains are five minutes apart. Thankfully our next-door neighbor is with her. She can't stay long, though, as she has a commitment later this afternoon."

"Is she heading to the hospital soon?" Avery knew next to nothing about labor pains or when Lilly should consider getting medical help.

"Not yet," he told her. "She called her OB-GYN and she said to wait until the pains are closer together."

"That's good, right?"

He nodded.

"I'm sure you'll make it to the hospital in time." Seeing that there was little she could do to relieve his worry, she did her best to sound positive.

"I appreciate your assurance." He rubbed his fingers through his already disheveled hair.

"If you need anything, let us know."

"Thanks, but I doubt there's much anyone can do at this point. Lilly and I took birthing classes, so we know what to expect. It's early yet. On our last doctor's visit, she said the baby should arrive right on time. Now this. From what your friend said, this is early stages, right? So even if the repairs take another couple hours, I should make it to the hospital in plenty of time for the birth."

"That's reassuring," Avery said, although James didn't sound the least bit confident.

Harrison got up and walked to the cafeteria. He returned in short order and handed James a cup of coffee. "I thought you might need this."

"Thanks, man. I appreciate it."

Harrison accepted James's gratitude. "You're going to need the caffeine, as it's bound to be a long day and night."

James grinned as he tasted the hot coffee.

"Do you know if you're having a boy or a girl?" Avery asked.

James shook his head. "We decided we wanted to be surprised."

"Names?" Avery asked next.

"Nicholas for a boy and Noelle for a girl. We wanted to keep it simple and in line with the holiday. Lilly's due date is January fifth . . . If the baby is born early, we'll get a tax deduction," he added.

"Everything is going to be fine," Harrison said and turned to Avery, seemingly about to ask her something, when Olivia approached, skipping, with a big smile.

"Hello, Olivia," Avery said cheerfully. It must be difficult for the little girl to be confined for hours on end.

"Hello." She looked at Harrison. "Is he your boyfriend?"

"Not yet," Harrison answered before Avery had a chance to. "But I'm working on it."

Olivia laughed. "You're silly."

"Yes, he is," Avery agreed, and frowned at Harrison.

If she noticed, Olivia didn't say anything. "I want you to come and meet my daddy. He was on the ferry. Mommy and I didn't even know it."

Avery glanced over to where Beth sat. Sure enough, there was a man in the seat beside her. The two sat stiffly, looking straight ahead.

"Can you come?" Olivia asked, and held out her hand to Avery.

"Sure thing." Avery stood and followed the girl back to where she had first sat before moving to be near Harrison.

"Daddy, Daddy," Olivia said, tugging Avery closer.

"Yes, pumpkin," he said, smiling at Olivia.

"I want you to meet my new friend. She has a pretty name. It's Avery."

"Logan Sullivan." Logan stood and exchanged handshakes with Avery.

"I'm so sorry," Beth interjected. "Is Olivia pestering you again?"

"Not in the least," Avery was quick to tell her. "I was sitting around waiting like everyone else."

"I didn't realize Olivia had wandered off."

"No problem." Avery brushed off Beth's concern. "Like I said, I wasn't doing anything important."

"My daddy is going to spend Christmas with us," Olivia explained excitedly. "Mommy called my grandma and grandpa, and Grandma said Daddy was welcome. Now I don't need to see Santa, because I already have what I really wanted and that was my daddy to be with us for Christmas!"

Logan frowned and then looked away.

Olivia's happy face melted as she glanced at her father. "Daddy is going to Seattle to sell his motorcycle. He promised to give me a ride one day, but I don't know how he can if he sells it."

"Pumpkin," Logan said, gently chastising his daughter. "It's impolite to tell people someone else's personal business."

With an apologetic look, Olivia placed both her hands over her mouth. "I'm sorry."

"It's okay," Avery whispered to Olivia and smiled at Beth and Logan, "I won't tell anyone."

Olivia's face brightened. "This is going to be the very best Christmas ever."

Avery hoped it would be, for Olivia's sake.

CHAPTER EIGHT

Virginia spent an entire hour seething after her last text from her twin. She should have known that despite her effort to build a bridge, Veronica was determined to make this as uncomfortable as possible. Regret filled her. She was sorry she'd even tried to make peace. It was more than apparent that her sister had no regrets and didn't feel a need for reconciliation.

Even in the season of goodwill and peace for mankind, her twin had turned her back on Virginia. Fine and well. This would be the last time Virginia made the attempt to heal their differences. The next effort, if there was one, would need to come from Veronica. Virginia was finished. She'd had enough. Christmas or not.

It demanded every iota of common sense she possessed to resist the urge to throw the entire tin of cookies overboard. It struck her then that rather than toss the double batch of gingerbread men, she should share them with the others. The cafeteria was out of food and there were sure to be hungry people who would appreciate all the love and care that had gone into baking these cookies.

Opening the tin, she noticed Olivia closely watching her. When the little girl spied the cookies, her eyes lit up with delight.

"Would you like one?" Virginia asked, lifting the tin for Olivia to get a better view.

She nodded eagerly and looked to her mother for permission. Beth smiled and agreed that Olivia could help herself.

The little girl jumped down from her seat and stared inside the tin box as if having a hard time deciding which one to take. "They're all so pretty."

"They taste even better than they look," Virginia told her, noting the youngster's appreciation.

Olivia reached for the top one. She broke off the head and ate. "They are so good. Thank you."

"You're most welcome. Would you like to do me a favor?"

"Yes," Olivia agreed eagerly.

"Would you go around and offer a cookie to each

passenger?" she asked. "That is, if your mom says it's all right."

"Olivia would enjoy that," Beth said. "But are you sure you want to give all your cookies away?" Beth looked astonished at Virginia's generosity.

"People are hungry" was all she said. Virginia handed the tin over to Olivia, who immediately headed in the direction of the group of musicians. Each one claimed a cookie and Olivia pointed back to Virginia. The men waved their gratitude.

Olivia went from group to group and the grumbling gradually turned to calls of appreciation.

What Virginia didn't expect was that her act of defiance against her sister would have such a positive effect. Soon others brought out and shared their own supply of goods. There were popcorn balls, chocolates, and even dill pickles passed around. The mood shifted from discontent to a camaraderie that had been missing earlier.

The band brought up their instruments and started to play, which helped to lighten the mood tremendously.

Virginia couldn't believe the change. It was as if the delay, as miserable as it was, had now brought everyone together. No one was happy, but there was acceptance that they were all together in this and needed to make the best of the situation.

Her own mood lightened until Virginia's thoughts returned to her twin.

Being trapped on this ferry made it impossible for Virginia to return to the Kitsap Peninsula. Her only option was to continue to Seattle.

Her phone dinged, indicating she had another text. Before she read the note, she sensed it was from her twin.

I'm still waiting to hear how long you will be delayed.

Virginia fumed and nearly tossed her phone back inside her purse. After a few uncomfortable moments while she fussed in her chair, she decided to answer.

You didn't answer my question.

The response was immediate.

What question? I don't recall you asking me a question.

Blowing out an irritated sigh, Virginia shook her head. How convenient for Veronica to pretend she didn't know what she was talking about.

I asked if you wanted me to come or not, Virginia reminded her. She hesitated, her finger lingering over the phone, before deciding not to add that she regretted the entire effort she'd made. In the end, she left it unsaid.

Yes.

Yes, what?

Yes, I still want you to come.

She did? Virginia read the note three times, uncertain how she should feel. In her own way, Veronica was reaching out to her, she supposed, although she wasn't completely sure. Some of the anger she'd experienced minutes earlier dissipated.

You're still delayed?

I didn't want to drive in this weather and decided to take the ferry. It broke down and now we're stuck in the middle of Puget Sound.

Once again, the reply was fast in coming, almost instantaneous.

You're on THAT ferry? It's been on the news. The reporter said no one knows how long the wait will be.

Just my luck. Trust me, no one on board is happy about this. We're making the best of it, though.

I can only imagine.

If there's an update about our situation, the television stations might get to hear about it before we do. I'd appreciate it if you'd let me know.

Of course. I'm relieved.

Relieved? That was odd.

Never mind. It was nothing.

Hmm, Virginia found that to be an interesting comment.

Without knowing how long this is going to take, will it interrupt your plans for later? she asked.

Plans?

Earlier you mentioned you had a commitment later and if I couldn't tell you how long it would be that it would be best if I didn't come. Remember?

It still hurt, and she hoped her twin could read between the lines and know how offended she'd been.

Veronica took several moments before she responded. Virginia held on to her phone so tightly her fingers ached as she awaited another text.

I was afraid telling me you were delayed was because you'd changed your mind.

No, I was being completely honest.

I see that now.

What about your commitment?

Not being able to give her sister a timeline for her visit made her situation difficult.

Another lengthy delay.

There isn't one.

That Veronica was willing to admit to the lie was promising. She smiled and the stiffness left her shoulders and her neck as she relaxed.

Then I'll take an Uber directly to your house as soon as we dock.

With Mom's gingerbread cookies?

About those cookies, I handed them out when the cafeteria ran out of food. I hope you don't mind.

Of course I don't mind. That was a thoughtful thing to do.

Virginia had to smile. If only her sister knew what had prompted her generosity.

The cookies were a hit, she typed.

No doubt. Mom's gingerbread always is. I can't wait to see you. Later, then, Veronica texted.

Later, Virginia texted back, smiling the entire time.

CHAPTER NINE

Kellie felt like a kid again. Reed had suggested they ride Seattle's Big Wheel, something she'd always wanted to do. Like so many other things, this was one of those fun ideas that was far too easy to put off until *someday*. It looked like *someday* had finally arrived and she was thrilled. This afternoon, as they lazily strolled down the festive waterfront, the sights and sounds of the holidays were all around them, wrapping her in a spirit of joy she hadn't felt in months.

Eventually, after several short stops along the way, Reed went to purchase their tickets, and learned there was a two-hour wait time for the Ferris wheel. She shouldn't have been surprised. This was one of the most popular tourist spots in town, along with the Space Needle and the tour of Underground Seattle.

Reed handed her the tickets. "Are you sure we'll have enough time? I mean, the ferry should be working by then, don't you think?"

"Maybe," he said. "And maybe not. That call from my sister indicated the problem could take several hours to fix. Nothing ventured, nothing gained, right?"

"Right," she agreed. As eager as she was to see her brother, she found herself happy to spend what she could of this day with Reed.

"Seeing that we've got a wait, let's explore Pike Place Market," Reed suggested.

"What a great idea." They headed up what is known in Seattle as the Pike Street Hill Climb, the 163 stairs leading from the waterfront to Pike Place Market. Their progress was slow, as the popular walkway was congested.

As they reached the top a bit breathless, Reed tucked her hand in the crook of his elbow. As if expecting her to object, he added, "In case you lose your footing again."

Kellie was more than happy to hold on to him, especially in the crowd of holiday shoppers that filled the market with its multiple stalls. The entire area was alive with activity. Although she'd lived in the Seattle area for several years, Kellie had been to Pike Place Market only a handful of times. It never failed to fascinate her. The market, like Seattle Center, was the heart of the city. It pulsed with charm and an old-world vibe.

Upon entering, they paused outside the seafood display. A bed of crushed ice showed a variety of halibut, salmon, tuna, rockfish, crab, oysters, and clams, all fresh from the waters of the Pacific Northwest.

While noting the wide array of fish, a large salmon went flying over her head to be caught by a fishmonger. A loud cheer went up, followed by a round of enthusiastic applause. Kellie had heard about the salmon toss, as it was a well-known tourist antic. Seeing it in person was a first, and she loved it.

From the fish stall, Reed steered them into the body of the market. The next place that caught Kellie's attention were the flower stands. Brightly colored large bouquets of blooms of every conceivable color were on display. Red carnations, gladioli, and roses were a few of the flowers Kellie could easily identify. Living in a condo close to her worksite, she wasn't into gardening other than a couple houseplants and a few herbs that grew on her windowsill. The bouquets were wrapped in holiday colors that were a feast for the eyes and the senses. Despite the cold, Kellie drew in a deep breath, hoping to catch a whiff of their fragrance.

"Look," she said, pausing to admire the beauty and artwork. "These arrangements are breathtaking."

"They are," Reed agreed. "You should have one." He immediately caught the attention of the Asian woman who sat on an upturned wooden crate, working on wrapping up the bouquets.

"Reed, no." Kellie reached for his forearm, stopping him. "I didn't mean for you to—"

"Let me do this as a small appreciation for saving me from a boring afternoon," Reed insisted. "Pick whichever one you like best."

Kellie hesitated. Each arrangement was so beautiful, it was difficult to choose. After looking over several, she pointed to one with sprigs of holly along with the red and white carnations and roses.

"That Christmas-looking one," she said, glancing back at Reed.

"Perfect."

The older woman named the price.

Kellie swallowed hard. She'd inadvertently chosen one of the priciest bunches available. She wanted to protest but didn't have the heart to disappoint Reed, as he seemed intent on purchasing her the flowers.

"Thank you," she said, being as gracious as she could and yet a bit reluctant. Reed had already paid for their lunch. When dating Jude, they'd always shared expenses. Kellie was accustomed to paying her way.

The shopkeeper wrapped the bouquet in newspaper and then in a clear bag before handing it to Kellie. She winked at her and whispered, "Hang on to him, dear, he's a keeper."

If Reed heard he pretended not to, for which Kellie was grateful.

"I'll carry it," he offered, taking the bouquet from her.

They continued down the packed corridor, working their way through the throng of shoppers and others like them simply enjoying the sights and sounds of the market. Passing a variety of meat and vegetable stands, they eventually edged to the stalls selling handcrafts and homemade specialties.

Kellie paused in front of the booth selling small figurines made from the ash of the Mount Saint Helen's volcano. "I think Harrison might appreciate this." Her brother was a history buff. The eruption happened in 1980 before either of them had been born and remained an important part of history for the Pacific Northwest. It amazed her, after all these years, that the ash was still readily available.

She chose a bear figurine, as her brother's high

school sports teams were known as the Grizzlies. Not that he participated in sports his senior year. Harrison would have been a great football player, except his low grades had kept him off the team. Harrison's lack of interest in academics had caused a rift between her brother and their father. Thankfully, that had changed after he'd enlisted in the Navy. She knew Harrison had a good relationship with their parents these days, and that pleased her.

Kellie paid, and Reed added the small paper bag into the one with the flowers.

The stall next door sold homemade jams and jellies. Reed paused there to read over the labels. "My sister loves spicy food. I bet she'd enjoy this raspberry-jalapeño jam."

"Perfect for Christmas Morning breakfast," Kellie agreed.

Reed added that to their sack along with their other purchases.

They left the market and discovered a Christmas bazaar across the street under a large white tent. With time to explore, they ventured inside. Kellie discovered a booth selling hand-spun yarn in a variety of enticing colors.

"Do you knit?" Reed asked.

"I did years ago while in college." Viewing the yarn

brought back a flood of warm memories. "I'd forgotten how much I enjoyed it. My roommate and I took up knitting, but that was years ago." She paused and stifled a laugh. "In an act of dedication and love, I decided to knit my college boyfriend a sweater."

"I hope he appreciated all the time and effort that went into the project."

Unable to hold back her amusement any longer, Kellie burst out laughing. "The sweater was a disaster. He was polite enough to thank me, but he never wore it, and I don't blame him. I believe it ended up lining his dog's bed."

Reed chuckled.

"I haven't knit anything since then. I still have my knitting needles, although I have no idea where I tucked them away." She picked up a skein of light brown yarn.

The young woman at the booth said, "Feel how soft it is? This yarn comes from Tinkerbell, one of my favorite sheep. I blended her wool with cashmere, which is why it's so soft."

Pressing the yarn against her cheek, Kellie had to agree. It was amazingly soft and pliable.

"There's enough yardage to knit up a hat or a pair of fingerless gloves," the young sheep herder/yarn dyer pressed.

Simply holding the yarn in her hands gave Kellie the

urge to take up knitting again. "It's been years since I held a pair of needles."

"Knitting is like riding a bike," the young woman assured her. "It's a skill we don't lose or forget."

"I don't really have anyone in my life who needs a hat. My brother doesn't like hats and . . ."

She chanced a look at Reed. "I don't suppose you could use a hat, could you?"

His eyes widened and he quickly nodded. "I'd love it if you'd knit me a hat, and I promise not to let it become part of my dog's bed."

"Do you have a dog?"

"Not yet."

"Then that's an easy promise," she teased.

"I offer a free hat pattern," the woman said, encouraging the sale. "And I can recommend a knitting group sponsored by a local yarn store if you run into any trouble."

Kellie couldn't keep from smiling. "Sold." She quickly paid before she could change her mind. The woman handed her the yarn, and the pattern, which Reed added to their small bag of treasures.

As they strolled away, Kellie asked, "You were joking about me knitting you that hat, right?"

Reed shook his head. "I was serious. How long do you think it will take you?"

"I have no idea." Already doubts were setting in. She'd bought the yarn on impulse and wondered if she'd wasted her money.

"I'll hold the yarn for you to roll," he offered. "I did that for my grandmother when I was a kid. Grandma knit Avery and me a sweater every Christmas. Knitting for her was an act of love . . ." He paused, as if he realized what he'd said. "Not that . . . Well, never mind." He started turning red.

"I understand, Reed. I'll be happy to knit you a hat and have you hold the skein while I unwind it." If she was reading him correctly, Reed was basically telling her that this day wouldn't be the last time they saw each other. Caught up in the spirit of Christmas, with all the fun festivities taking place around them, Kellie had fallen under the spell of the holidays.

As much as she liked Reed, and she truly did, she wasn't convinced she was ready for another relationship. Her heart remained bruised. Jude had done a number on her, and she was hesitant to get involved again, especially with someone who worked at Microsoft.

"You're looking thoughtful," Reed said.

"Just thinking," she said. Without the protection of the market, the wind whipped around them. Already the sky was showing signs of darkening. By four o'clock it would be nearly completely dark. A chill raced up her arms.

"Are you cold?" he asked.

"A little," she admitted.

"I could use a cup of coffee, how about you?"

"That sounds like a great idea."

Reed took her hand. "The original Starbucks is just down the street."

"Do we have time?" she asked, referring to the ticket time for the Ferris wheel.

"We should have. It depends on how busy they are," he said.

As expected, the line to get into the original Starbucks was out the door. They took their place on the sidewalk. This was likely the most popular of all the Starbucks because of its history. Tourists loved claiming they'd bought coffee at the very first Starbucks.

Reed grew quiet as well. "I apologize, Kellie," he said. He stood behind her and his voice was close to her ear.

"Sorry?" She turned to face him, not understanding.

"I'm coming on too strong, aren't I?"

"What do you mean?"

"I think I might have been a little too eager for you to knit me that hat because I want to see you again."

"Reed," she said, stopping him. She placed her hand

on his arm. "You should know I came out of a long-term relationship a while ago and I'm a little hesitant. We've only just met—well, met again. Besides, if you remember, I was the one who offered to knit you that hat. The fact is, I'm looking forward to unearthing my knitting needles."

He grinned and seemed to relax. "Then you should know I enjoy spending time with you. I hope we can do it again soon."

"I'm having a great time myself."

The line slowly moved forward. "When I saw you at the ferry terminal," he said, "I thought . . ." He hesitated, as if he wasn't sure he should continue.

"What did you think?" she prodded. The line moved again, and she walked backward, her gaze holding his.

"I thought, there is a woman I would like to know better. A woman of intelligence and beauty. I'm not good at relationships. Hard as I try, I mess them up, and half the time I don't even know what I did wrong."

"Is it because of the traveling?"

He shrugged. "It doesn't help that I'm frequently away a week or more at a time. I've thought about transferring to a different department or even finding another position that would allow me to work from a single location. The problem, if you can call it a problem, is that I thoroughly enjoy what I do. There's a deep sense of satisfaction in getting an entire company up and running with the latest software development."

Kellie understood the importance of his position in the company. "It's valuable work and part of what the customers expect if they are investing millions of dollars in our products."

"It's great that you understand and can appreciate my role." The relief on his face was endearing.

They made their way inside the door and reached the counter within a few minutes. The barista took their order, then placed a label on their cups before handing them off. They stepped aside to the waiting area for their order to be finished. It didn't take long for their coffees to be placed on the counter.

Reed glanced at his wrist. "Oh boy," he murmured.

"Oh boy?" she repeated, taking a sip of her drink. "What does that mean?"

"We only have five minutes to make it back to the Ferris wheel."

"Five minutes?"

"Five minutes. How fast can you run?"

"Run?" she repeated, feeling like a parrot repeating everything he said. "I sit at a desk all day. I do water aerobics, not marathons."

"Do you want to ride the Ferris wheel or save it for another time?"

"Today is the day. I'm game if you are."

Grabbing hold of her hand, he maneuvered their way past those blocking the door and raced toward the waterfront.

They reached the wheel in the nick of time and were the last ones to board.

Kellie was breathless as they took their seats. She pressed her hand over her heart and expelled a long sigh before she burst out laughing.

"What's so funny?" Reed asked.

"Us," she said between giggles. "We looked like a pair of felons escaping the police." She took in another stabilizing breath as Reed started to laugh himself.

He looked at her and smiled.

Kellie smiled back. "This is the most fun I've had since I don't know when."

"Me, too," he agreed.

"I'm happy it was with you."

His smile grew even bigger. "I was thinking the same thing."

CHAPTER TEN

Beth kept a close eye on Olivia as her daughter bounced around the deck, visiting with passengers here and there. Because she was naturally open and friendly, people responded with smiles and short conversations.

Even though they hadn't talked much, she noticed a marked difference in Logan after he answered a text. She couldn't see what was said and mentally chastised herself for sneaking a peek. It seemed like it had something to do with the sale of his motorcycle.

Looking up from his phone, Logan centered his focus on Olivia, briefly smiled, and said, "She's really something, isn't she?"

Her daughter was the very light that brightened

Beth's world. "She is," Beth agreed, "and like you in so many ways."

"Me?" Logan challenged with a short, disbelieving laugh.

"You don't see it?" Beth had a hard time not recognizing Logan's qualities in their child. "She's intelligent . . ."

Her husband snickered. "You seem to forget I didn't have the smarts to graduate from college."

"You took the courses that most interested you, though."

"They were tough. I knew next to nothing about marketing and management . . . I don't know if I'd have stuck it out if not for you."

Beth denied that with a sharp shake of her head. "I don't believe that for a minute. Your mind was set to make the best of each class long before we met. Most likely you were bored in high school, which is why you received such poor grades." She didn't know that for a fact, although it made sense. Logan was a whiz with numbers and excelled in all his math classes. His hope was one day to start his own construction company. Life, however, had gotten in the way. That dream must feel impossible in their current situation.

"I always found it difficult to sit still," he elaborated.

"Most of the subjects we studied didn't interest me in the least. All I ever wanted was . . ."

"Was what?" she pressed when he paused midsentence.

A long moment passed before he continued. "To make a good living and support a family," he said, lowering his head and his voice until it was little more than a whisper.

Logan had his dreams, ones he rarely spoke of any longer, which broke her heart. His dreams seemed to have wilted and died inside of him.

"Working construction is nothing to be ashamed of," Beth said, upset that he would downplay his skills.

"When there's work, you mean."

"We're getting off the subject," Beth said, disliking the path their conversation was heading in. "We were talking about Olivia, remember."

"Right."

"You're good with your hands and so is she. Olivia loves puzzles. I had one of those complicated five-hundred-piece ones out on the dining room table. It was a Christmas scene of the manger with Joseph, Mary, baby Jesus, and all the barn animals, with angels looking down on them. Five hundred small pieces. Olivia worked on it nearly every day after school. I was afraid it would be too hard for her, but she insisted she could do it and she did."

"She completed the puzzle?"

"Not yet. I'll admit, though, that she's found more pieces than I have by two to one. She gets her patience and persistence from you, Logan."

He responded with a fleeting smile, and then he quickly drew serious. "I've missed being with her, seeing her bright smile every day."

Beth bit back the urge to remind him that he was the one who chose to leave. He faithfully spent time with Olivia every other Saturday, unless he was working, and called often to speak to her. It wasn't the same, though, as him coming home each night, sharing the everyday nuances of their daughter's life. And hers, too.

She realized their real problem was the lack of communication. When she hid her parents' financial help, that had served to feed Logan's feelings of inadequacy. Instead of the two of them talking it out, coming to a solution together to repay her family, she'd cooked his favorite meals and did all she could to pretend everything was normal. She wasn't the only one at fault. Logan had clammed up, becoming uncommunicative. How she wished things could be different.

"That friendly nature she has is all you," Logan

said, interrupting her thoughts. "She's never met a stranger, has she?"

"No, never," Beth agreed.

Currently Olivia was visiting with Virginia, excitedly telling the older woman how much everyone enjoyed Virginia's cookies. The two of them were close enough for Beth to hear snatches of the conversation. The grandmother was telling Olivia that she had a granddaughter around Olivia's age and that she was taking the ferry to visit her twin sister. Olivia immediately had questions about her sister. There were a pair of twins in her class at school, a boy and a girl.

Logan must have caught part of the conversation, too. "Listen, I probably should have said something earlier."

"About?"

He hesitated. "I appreciate the invite, but I don't think it's a good idea for me to join you and your parents for Christmas. They might say they are okay with me joining you. That's just the kind of family you have; they are a blessing, but I'd feel out of place and weird dropping by . . . I don't belong, Beth. I'm sorry, I really am."

"What do you mean you don't belong? You're my husband, whether you want to claim me as your wife or not," she whispered fiercely, not wanting Olivia to overhear. This news would crush their daughter. All she really wanted for Christmas was for her daddy to be with her.

"I'm not going to argue with you, Beth. I don't belong. It'll be awkward for everyone. You don't need that on Christmas."

"It won't be . . ." She wanted to argue, but before she could say another word, Logan continued.

"You should have made a better choice in a husband. It's time you accepted that and moved on."

Beth folded her arms and stiffened at his words. Her throat thickened and she was afraid to speak for fear the tears would leak into her voice. After several awkward moments she felt composed enough to respond.

"You're right, Logan, I do deserve better. When we married, I believed in you. In us. I felt that no matter what the future held, we would face it together . . . that the love we shared, the home we built, would see us through any storm. I was wrong, though, wasn't I?"

He didn't answer, not that she expected he would.

"I got pregnant with Olivia, and when I told you, you freaked out," she added.

"We weren't financially ready for a family," he reminded her, as if this was news she hadn't realized.

"Who is ever ready? We talked about starting a family and we kept putting it off. I didn't get pregnant on purpose. I was on birth control, and while you might think our daughter was an accident, she is anything but that. She is my entire world."

"I love Olivia, too," he insisted. "More than anything."

"Deep down I believe that, which is why I find it so difficult to understand why you walked away from us. Is it me you can't love?" Despite every effort, tears leaked from her eyes and rolled down her cheeks. She was sick of his silence. Sick of him leaving her to face life alone instead of them standing tall together, supporting each other. Sick of all the lonely nights she spent longing for her husband.

"How can you say I don't love you? I pay support every month, and let me tell you, it isn't easy. I've sacrificed so much for Olivia and for you. I've gone without lunches and made do with worn-out work clothes."

Beth was tempted to remind him of all the things she'd done without, too, but remained silent.

"I live in a basement a friend is renting me that is cold and dank to make sure you and Olivia have what you need," he continued.

"You're right, you meet your obligations," she agreed, both angry and hurt. "But don't you see how much Olivia idolizes you? How much she misses you?

Didn't you notice how excited she was to see that you were here on the ferry? What do you think she's telling people?" she asked, and gestured to Olivia excitedly chatting with Virginia.

Before he could answer, she responded for him. "Olivia is letting everyone know her father is going to spend Christmas with her. All she wants is time with you, time with her daddy."

Several uncomfortable moments passed before he spoke. "Like I said earlier, I'm not the man for you. I'm a rotten husband and an even worse father."

The urge to argue was hard to hold back. He'd been a good husband until he'd learned her parents had helped with Olivia's medical expenses.

Logan had always stressed about finances, and the future. Each month he grew more and more depressed, especially when they ran out of money for key items such as electricity and groceries. Beth knew it was wrong not to tell Logan her parents had paid off the medical bills. Because she was a stay-at-home mom, she paid the bills each month. They reviewed them together, deciding how best to budget their income. She hid the fact that the medical bills had been paid, knowing how upset it would make him. It didn't take long for Logan to figure it out when there was suddenly enough money for a few extras they had done without for years.

Instead of being grateful, he'd taken her parents' help as a slight against his manhood and his ability to support his family.

From that moment forward, it felt like Logan gave up on them. Since they split, it seemed like he'd set out to prove that she could have made a better choice in a husband and a father for Olivia.

Neither spoke for a long time.

Skipping with her pigtails bobbing, Olivia approached her father. "Do you want to draw a picture with me?" she asked Logan, oblivious to the tension between them.

Beth turned to stare at Logan. If he turned Olivia down after everything she'd just said, she didn't know if she could remain quiet. He was already determined to disappoint her by not sharing Christmas with them.

"I'm not good at drawing," Logan said reluctantly.

"That's all right," Olivia said, unwilling to accept his excuse. "I can show you how to draw a reindeer. I learned how in my art class at school. I do it really good."

"I bet you do," Logan said. "But I don't have any pencils or paper."

"I can get it for us. See that boy over there. His name is Kevin and he's eight. His mom brought some stuff to keep him entertained, so he has paper and colored pencils. His mother said they would be happy to share." She looked expectantly at her father.

After what felt like an eternity to Beth, he said, "Okay, pumpkin, you can teach me to draw a reindeer."

Olivia's face burst into a huge smile as she raced across the room to where Kevin sat with his parents.

"That wasn't so hard now, was it?" Beth felt obliged to say.

Logan glared back at her.

In return, she ignored the sarcastic look and smiled sweetly.

One of the small tables in the cafeteria area was available. Logan stood and claimed it before anyone else could.

Once Olivia collected the supplies from her newfound friend Kevin, she joined her father, taking the seat next to him, intent on showing him how good of an artist she was.

With a hard lump of pain tightening her stomach, Beth's gaze focused on father and daughter. When they'd first happened upon Logan, she'd been overwhelmed. It'd been so long since she'd last had more than a brief conversation with her husband.

Foolishly, she'd been filled with hope that somehow Christmas would work its magic and they would find a way to overcome their problems. Apparently, miracles were in short supply this year.

That Logan would disappoint Olivia over Christmas broke her heart. Beth didn't know if it was in her to forgive him again, not when her parents had been willing to look past the hurt he'd caused and welcome him into their home. Perhaps it was time to move forward and accept that their marriage was over. She hated to admit defeat. Making a go of it, though, with Logan's attitude, would be impossible.

Logan and Olivia sat at the table working on their drawings. Every now and again, Olivia would let out a laugh and shake her head. At one point she grabbed Logan's paper and ran to show Beth.

"Look at what Daddy drew," she said, her expression full of joy. "Isn't he silly?"

The sketch was of a reindeer face on a man's body.

Beth did her best to smile. "Your daddy is silly, isn't he?"

"He draws good, too."

"Yes, he does," Beth agreed.

Logan and Olivia sat together for several minutes longer. While the pair were occupied, Beth decided to fill her mother in on this latest development, this latest hurt.

Logan glanced up and noticed she had her phone to

her ear. He seemed to know exactly who she'd called. Her mother answered quickly, and after a short exchange of greetings, Beth said, "I don't think Logan will come for Christmas after all," she murmured, talking past the lump in her throat.

"He won't?" Surprise came with the question. "Whatever happened to change his mind?"

"I . . . I don't know. Olivia was so excited. This news is going to crush her." Beth was convinced even the iPad her parents had purchased for her daughter wouldn't take away the sting of Logan's decision.

"Would it help if I talked to him?" her mother volunteered. "I'm sure he's hesitating because he thinks it will be uncomfortable with him here. If I could reassure him your father and I hold no hard feelings, perhaps he'll change his mind."

If she thought it would do any good, Beth would agree. "I appreciate the offer, Mom, but Logan has already made up his mind."

Her mother sympathized. "I'm sorry, sweetheart."

"I am, too." She didn't bother to hide her pain. She wanted to cry and shout at Logan; he needed to know how much it hurt. He filled them both with such hope, only to dash it all away in a single moment. It was like he had no heart. Not even at Christmas.

They talked a bit longer and then disconnected. A

stray tear rolled down Beth's cheek. It all felt so hopeless. All these months she'd lived with the idea that perhaps she and Logan could manage to find a way back to each other. She hadn't filed for a divorce, claiming neither one could afford an attorney. The time to be realistic was long past due. Nothing was going to change as badly as she wanted it to, as much as she desired for them to be a family again. She brushed away the tear before Olivia saw that she was upset.

Eager to show her mother her artwork, Olivia ran to her mom and Beth forced a smile. "Show me your picture," she said, doing her best to keep her voice light and airy.

Her daughter handed her a sheet with several reindeer faces along with a Christmas tree and a wreath. "Good job," Beth praised Olivia's efforts.

"That's what Daddy said. He did good, too."

Beth nodded.

With her shoulders drooping, Olivia added, "Daddy said he wanted to sit over there instead of here with us now."

"Okay," Beth said, not the least bit surprised. "Stay here and watch our things. I need to tell your dad something."

"Okay," Olivia said. "Will he come sit with us again, do you think?"

"I don't know . . . Maybe." She didn't have the heart to tell her daughter the truth.

Leaving Olivia to stand guard was the only way she could avoid her daughter hearing their conversation.

Logan looked up as she approached, wearing a frown.

She reassured him right away. "Don't worry, I'm not going to ask you to come sit with us."

Relief showed in his eyes.

"After telling Olivia that you'd be with us on Christmas Day, you've now decided to disappoint our daughter. All I ask is that you be man enough to tell her instead of leaving it up to me. That's the least you can do."

With that, Beth returned to where Olivia waited, looking up expectantly. Seeing that it was only her mother and not Logan, the little girl's face fell.

CHAPTER ELEVEN

Logan was sick at heart. He'd been excited to see Beth and Olivia on the ferry. At first, he'd been shocked, and wary, too. His heart had leapt with a sense of joy to find the two people he loved more than life itself on this ferry. He'd had no idea they were headed into Seattle or that he'd unexpectedly run into them.

He'd been heading to Seattle to sell his motorcycle. He loved that machine and drove it to work most days, as it was far more economical than his truck. His old pickup was a gas guzzler. And then one of the men on his crew who lived close by had agreed to give Logan a ride to and from work. That had its advantages and disadvantages.

The biggest advantage was that by selling his bike,

he'd be able to give Olivia and Beth a Christmas gift. He desperately wanted them to know how deeply he loved them. He'd failed at most everything when it came to his wife and daughter, so the least he could do was show them he cared enough to buy them a Christmas present.

Now that would be impossible. The entire reason he'd been on this doomed ferry was to meet the buyer who'd contacted him. The plan was for Logan to bring over the bike for him to examine. If the guy found the motorcycle to his liking, he'd pay the agreed-upon price. Logan would take an Uber back to the dock and ride the ferry home.

And now his plan had gone awry with the ferry stalled in the water. He'd reached out to let the buyer know he'd be late for the appointment time they'd set. The text reply told Logan that the guy's wife had talked him out of buying a motorcycle, claiming it was too dangerous.

Logan felt his heart sink to his stomach to the point that he felt physically ill. With only two days until Christmas, he wouldn't be able to find another buyer in time to purchase any gifts.

When he'd agreed to spend Christmas with Beth's parents, he'd envisioned arriving with a bottle of fine

Scotch for Grant, Beth's father, and a poinsettia for Irene, her mother. He already had a beautiful piece of jewelry picked out for Beth. Something exquisite and delicate like his wife. He'd seen a cameo at the farmer's market and instantly knew it would be the perfect Christmas present for her. The woman who manned the stall had agreed to set it aside for him. Logan knew Beth would cherish that cameo.

But like so much else in life, it wasn't meant to be. With less than twenty bucks in his pocket, twenty bucks that would need to see him to the end of the month, now there would be nothing for Beth and Olivia.

With his shoulders hunched forward, he sat in the small cafeteria, his heart as heavy as it had ever been. For just a few hours he'd been filled with hope. With joy that he would be able to surprise his family with gifts that showed his heart.

He should have known better, should have realized that what his father said all those years ago was true.

Logan was no good, filled with lofty dreams that were doomed to fail.

Life hadn't been easy after his mother walked out. She'd left, kissed each of her two sons good-bye, and said she'd be in touch once she'd settled down. She would send for them, she'd said, and he'd believed her.

In the next three years Logan got one phone call and one birthday card and then nothing. That had been the extent of her interest and her love.

The first and only time she'd called was to let Logan know she'd found a job in a tavern and was putting aside her tips. It shouldn't take her more than a month or two to save up enough to rent a decent apartment. Once she did, she'd send for both boys. Logan lived on that dream until it was impossible to hold on to any longer.

The fool that he was, Logan had desperately wanted to believe his mother meant what she'd said. He gripped hold of her promise with everything he had and trusted her words.

After several weeks and then months without any word, he gave up hope. She hadn't given him any information on where she'd settled or any way of contacting her. The number she used had been disconnected when he tried to call back. It took far longer than it should have for him to realize everything she'd said had been a bald-faced lie.

Perhaps at one time she'd believed she would follow through, although in retrospect he didn't think so. Most likely, it was a way to suppress her guilt for having abandoned her sons.

With his mother gone, the situation at home got

worse. His father's drinking increased to the point that he was drunk most days. As a result, he grew more and more verbally aggressive.

Paul, Logan's younger brother, left before he did, running off in the middle of the night with a friend who had a car. He stole the secret stash Logan had saved. Logan had worked odd jobs before and after school, hoping that once he graduated, he could find his own escape.

Instead, he was stuck with an abusive father who gave up on life and, sadly, gave up on himself. In his misery, he took out his anger on Logan. Not physically, because by this time, Logan was taller and stronger than his father. He was smart enough not to try. The verbal abuse was worse than anything physical his father might have done, though.

More times than Logan could count, his father had reiterated that Logan didn't have any better chance of making something of himself than he had. Like his father, Logan was destined to fail at life.

His father's taunts echoed in his dreams, echoed in his marriage, and followed him into every endeavor since.

Heart and soul, he loved Beth and Olivia, but deep down he'd convinced himself they would be better off without him. They'd met while he was taking night classes at Seattle Community College. The minute he saw her, he knew she was everything he'd ever wanted. When Beth had agreed to marry him, he'd felt like the luckiest man alive. He'd been determined to be the best husband and father there was. God knew he tried. The picture he had in his mind was of a man who took care of his family, who made the most of life. A man with a construction business, building homes for families, creating communities. Those dreams were dust.

He longed to be a man like Grant Walsh, Beth's father.

When he'd met Beth's parents and siblings, he realized this was the kind of family he'd hoped for them to build together one day. He admired her father, looked up to him, wanted to emulate him.

"Daddy, Daddy," Olivia said, coming to stand in front of him, placing her hand on his.

He managed a weak smile when he glanced up at his beautiful daughter, his heart so full of love it was hard to hold back tears.

"What is it, pumpkin?"

"Can you come sit with Mommy and me again? I liked it when you were closer."

Logan's gaze drifted over to where Beth sat, her back stiff, her disappointment in him coming off her in waves of discontent.

"I'm sorry," he whispered, feeling defeated and utterly miserable.

Olivia didn't pout or complain. Instead, she gave a sad shake of her head and returned to her mother.

Feeling low and dejected, Logan watched her go.

CHAPTER TWELVE

Avery was so intent on her conversation with Harrison that she hardly noticed the time. She honestly tried to keep up her guard, not allowing herself to be taken in by his charm and wit. Increasingly, she found it difficult. They continued with their question-and-answer session.

"Okay, what's your favorite dish?"

"A teacup," she joked.

"I meant food-wise. You know: Italian, Mexican, Chinese?"

"All of the above, plus Thai, Indian. And bread. Oh my goodness, it's my weakness, along with seafood. I'm not a picky eater. What about you?"

"I'm not fond of cheese."

"You don't love cheese? That's un-American. Cheese is . . . It's a basic food group. Does that mean you don't enjoy pizza?"

He shrugged. "I eat it on occasion." He frowned and then asked, "Does my lack of appreciation for cheese disqualify me as dating material?"

"I'm going to have to give that some thought," she said, enjoying teasing him.

"I have several other fine qualities, if you give me an opportunity to show you."

"You mean like patience with this stalled ferry?"

"Yup, but I'll admit spending time with you because of the delay comes as a bonus."

It felt that way to her, too.

There didn't appear to be any progress regarding the crippled ferry. Many of their fellow passengers had tried to make the best of the situation. But as time dragged on, the mood had started to change with the lack of any further information.

"Okay, my turn," she said. "Where do you see yourself in five years?"

Harrison didn't hesitate. "I want to continue my career in the Navy, take some college classes, and learn what I can about being a leader. I believe within the next couple years I might have the opportunity to become a master chief." He paused and glanced at her. "I hope within a few years to marry and start a family."

Knowing Harrison planned to continue his Navy career gave her pause. She looked away as she mulled over his answer, and James caught her attention. Like everyone else, he was understandably restless and fidgety. He didn't seem able to stay in one place for any length of time. He kept circling the outside deck a number of times, and always with his phone in hand.

When Captain Douglas's voice finally came with an update, James hurried back inside. The waiting area that had been filled with voices of frustration and discontent instantly went silent.

"I have good news to report. The necessary part has been located and is on its way."

For a moment, the room went silent and still before bursting into chatter, filled with complaints. Avery understood and, like everyone else, was upset.

"You mean to say they didn't even locate the part until now?" James cried as he rammed his fingers through his hair. He looked both despondent and angry at once. And he wasn't the only one.

Although the captain's voice was nearly drowned out, he continued.

"The part will be delivered shortly. Once again, I

apologize for the inconvenience, but I promise the fix will be an easy one, and we'll be on our way as soon as possible."

"I need to get off this ferry!" James stood and cried out in desperation.

"Listen, we all do!" a man close by shouted back, his voice raised in anger.

"You don't understand—" James argued.

He was cut off by a dozen others all shouting at once.

"What makes you think you're more important than anyone else?" was one of the questions Avery heard.

"No one wants to stay on this ferry a minute longer than necessary. The last thing we need is someone like you thinking they're more important than anyone else."

"Yeah, buddy, I have a wedding . . ."

"My family is waiting."

"I could lose my job because of this."

The barrage of harsh comments continued, to the point that James appeared to go pale. He slumped down in his seat, bent over, and buried his face in his knees.

Feeling bad for James, Avery considered explaining the situation. She stood, but before she could speak, Harrison placed his hand on her arm, stopping her. "Nothing you say will do any good."

"People don't get it," Avery said. "Don't you think

everyone would be more sympathetic if they knew about his wife?"

"I doubt it," Harrison countered. "This is an angry crowd; no one is going to listen to reason. Everyone wants off this ferry."

"Surely there's something that can be done?" Avery felt terrible for James, who so desperately needed to be with his wife. Her heart went out to him. Harrison was right, though. This crowd wasn't likely to care one way or another. Not in their present mood.

Harrison grew quiet, as he appeared to be thinking. "From what the captain said, the fix will be here soon. That means there will likely be a speedboat or some other means of water transportation coming to the ferry, right?"

Avery nodded, as she followed his train of thought. "And if there's a speedboat due to arrive, then it will need to return. You think it might be possible for James to ride back?"

"Exactly," Harrison said, grinning.

"Let's talk to him," Avery said, anxious to come up with a solution for James.

"We'll need to get the captain's permission, of course," Harrison continued, thinking out loud, "but once he hears the circumstances, I have to believe he'll agree, don't you think?"

"I don't know why he wouldn't." Avery was excited. Harrison's idea might well work.

Avery moved to the empty seat to the right of James and Harrison took the one to the left. Harrison spoke, keeping his voice low.

"James, listen, Avery and I have an idea."

The expectant father raised his head. "Will it get me off this ferry?"

"It just might," Avery told him and squeezed his arm.

They had his full attention now. "Then tell me; I'm open to just about anything."

Harrison glanced around to be sure others weren't listening in on their conversation. "Perhaps it would be best if we spoke outside, where there aren't a lot of ears."

James hurried to his feet. "Okay. Sure."

The three of them moved to the outside deck. Avery wasn't prepared for the icy wind that buffeted against her. Seagulls floated in the breeze above them, and the angry dark clouds mirrored the mood of those impatiently awaiting rescue. She held on to the railing while Harrison explained their plan.

"Whoever delivers the part will likely return to Seattle once it's on board, right?"

"Right," James echoed. It was then that he understood. His eyes widened and he nodded with enough vigor to nearly send his glasses flying. "But how—I mean, who will I need to talk to about this? It isn't like I can become a stowaway without anyone noticing."

"The captain would be the one to grant permission, we think," Harrison said.

James appeared more than ready to do whatever was necessary to find a way onto that boat. He started for the door that would take him back inside the ferry when he paused. Looking unsure, he said, "Come with me."

Harrison shared a look with Avery as if silently asking her if this was a good idea or not.

"We should," she said. "There's power in numbers, and we have to get the captain to listen." At least she hoped that was the case.

Once inside, Harrison led them to the stairs that descended to the car deck, which was mostly deserted now. Those who drove onto the ferry had apparently grown restless, cold, and bored sitting inside their vehicles.

"Do you know where we will find the captain?" James asked, looking around the car deck.

Avery had no idea why Harrison had taken them belowdecks when it was highly likely the captain would be on the bridge.

"We don't have access to the captain," he explained. "Our best bet is to find one of the crew and have him convince the captain to meet with us."

"Down here?" James asked, spreading out his arms and circling around. All any of them could see were empty cars lined up bumper to bumper.

"No, there," Harrison said, pointing to a doorway that stated CREW ONLY.

Relief showed on James's face as he sighed and nodded.

The three approached the door. James hesitated. "Should we knock?" Not waiting for a response, James politely tapped the door.

No one responded.

Harrison tried next, pounding against the door with his fist.

Avery nearly groaned when Earl Jones, the crew member that they had dealt with earlier, angrily threw open the door. When he saw the three of them, he rolled his eyes as if to say he'd had enough of their eternal griping.

"What now?" he demanded.

"We need to see the captain," James explained impatiently. "It's a matter of utmost importance."

"And why is that?" Earl challenged.

"I need to get off this ferry," James said.

"Listen, buddy, get in line with everyone else." He was about to close the door in their faces.

"Wait," Avery cried. "You don't understand." Irritated by Earl's attitude, she did her best to control her temper. To be fair, the entire crew had been dealing with complaints and hostility for the last two hours. What he didn't understand was that with James there were extenuating circumstances.

"My wife is in labor," James cried. "I need to be with her."

Earl remained silent for several long moments. Avery feared he was about to turn them down flat and insist they return to the passenger deck.

She sighed with relief when he said, "Wait here." He closed the door and left them standing in the cold. James paced impatiently for what felt like an eternity.

Avery was about to give up when Earl returned. "Listen, I tried my best."

This didn't sound promising. Avery was sure they weren't going to be given a chance when he continued. "The captain agreed to give you five minutes to make your case."

"Thank you," James said, perking up. "I can't tell you how much I appreciate this." The relief in his voice was evident.

"You aren't allowed on the bridge."

Avery already knew it was highly unlikely they would be escorted there.

"Captain Douglas will join you in a few minutes. You need to understand he has a lot on his plate."

"I do, I do," James assured him.

"This ferry breaking down is highly unusual," Earl said. "We're all frustrated and miserable and the captain isn't likely to make allowances for you unless you can convince him this is a matter of life and death."

James nodded. "My wife has had a difficult pregnancy . . . This is our first baby, and she's alone and terrified. So am I."

Earl listened. "Got it." Next, he glanced at Avery and Harrison. "I did what I could. The best of luck to you."

"Thank you," Avery said, grateful for Earl's efforts. She was willing to let his previous attitude slide, seeing how helpful he'd been.

The three remained standing on the car deck for several minutes before the captain appeared.

"Lester Douglas," he said, by means of an introduction. He immediately got to the point. "Earl says you have extenuating circumstances to leave the ferry. Let's hear it."

James swallowed hard as if his throat had gone dry. "My wife is in labor."

"Here? On the ferry?" His eyes widened with the question, and he seemed surprised that this was the first time he'd heard of it.

"No, no, she's in Seattle. I need to get to her. I explained to Earl earlier this hasn't been an easy pregnancy and she's alone. We don't have any family in the area. Her mother is due to fly here, but not until after the first of the year."

The captain listened intently.

"I understand someone is delivering the part to repair the engine. I was hoping—praying, actually—that you would let me return with that boat."

Captain Douglas considered the request, his mouth tight as he mulled over what were sure to be the consequences.

Avery could almost see the other man's mind whirling. "You must understand that if word gets out that I let you leave, there is likely to be a riot. From what the crew is telling me, tensions are riding high, with a lot of people furious about the situation."

"That's true," James said.

Avery appreciated that James wasn't willing to downplay the ugly mood of those trapped on the passenger deck.

"Sir, please, this is dire. I need to be with my wife."

"You say your wife is alone," Captain Douglas said, studying James closely.

"Not exactly . . . A neighbor is currently with her, but she has to leave for a family function in an hour or so."

"Good, then she has someone at her side for now."

"That's true, but she needs me. I'm her husband, the father of her child." He looked at Avery and Harrison as if they would help him explain how crucial it was for him to return with the speedboat.

"Has she been admitted to the hospital?" Captain Douglas asked next.

"Not yet . . . but . . ."

The captain stopped him. "I'm sorry, son, I can't allow a single passenger to depart while so many others are just as desperate to get to Seattle. Your leaving would be grossly unfair to everyone else."

The device attached to the captain's hip made a squeaking sound. He jerked it off his belt and pushed a button.

From the brief conversation between the captain and the crew member, Avery learned that the speedboat had pulled up alongside the ferry. The fix had arrived. That was good news. Hopefully the ferry would soon be on its way and James would be able to be with his wife.

The captain left abruptly and the three of them started up the stairwell to the passenger deck.

"It won't be long now," Avery said, hoping to reassure James.

"Right," he said without a lot of enthusiasm.

Once they returned to the passenger deck, Avery noticed people lined up against the windows, watching the part be delivered. A cheer rose, followed by a burst of applause. It seemed the mood instantly lightened.

Avery relaxed, too. Like everyone else, she was eager to get to Seattle. With the end of this debacle in sight, Avery sent her brother a text, letting him know it wouldn't be much longer now. She'd been pleasantly surprised that Reed had hung around town to greet her and help her make the uphill trek to his condo. Coincidentally, her brother had also found a companion to help pass the time. He seemed to be enjoying himself.

James stood at the window with several others, watching excitedly as the speedboat pulled away. A cheer rose once again.

Thinking it would be only a matter of minutes, Avery noticed a few people return to their cars. Others gathered their items together, preparing for the departure.

But then another forty minutes passed and the restlessness returned. By all that was right, they should be underway by now. The information they had received was that it would take only a few minutes to install the part. Yet the ferry remained dead in the water. No one needed to tell Avery or anyone else that this easy fix apparently wasn't so easy.

Something wasn't right.

People started mumbling among themselves, pacing and looking anxious, asking questions no one could answer.

Before long, Captain Douglas's voice came over the intercom.

"Unfortunately, I have discouraging news."

A cacophony of discord and frustration echoed through the waiting area.

"As many of you noticed, we received what we hoped would be an easy fix. It has since been determined there is more than this single problem. The engine crew is working diligently . . ."

Whatever else the captain had to say was drowned out by the loud boos and curses. As the roar of discontent slowly dissipated, James's phone rang.

Looking desperate, he grabbed it with both hands.

Avery watched as James listened. He instantly went

pale and looked at Avery and Harrison as if he didn't know what else to do.

"What is it?" she asked, moving to stand next to him.

"That was our neighbor," he said. "Lilly's water broke and they're heading to the hospital."

CHAPTER THIRTEEN

After their fun ride on the Ferris wheel, Reed and Kellie continued their lazy stroll along the waterfront with no real destination in mind. They walked almost to the point where the cruise ships docked. Come May and June there would be as many as nine cruise ships anchored in Seattle, most heading to the pristine waters of Alaska. Reed was enjoying himself. Spending what would have been a long, boring afternoon with Kellie had made this one of the best days he could remember in a long while. She was everything he'd imagined. Friendly, warm, charming, funny, and caring. Even from the brief interaction they'd shared months earlier, he'd found himself attracted to her. After one afternoon, he knew beyond a doubt he really wanted to spend more time with her.

As they continued walking, he checked his phone to make sure he hadn't missed a text from Avery. Nothing yet. Whatever the problem was with the engine, it must have been major. Earlier Avery had assured him that once the part arrived the ferry should be on its way in short order. Although he was warm in his thick wool jacket, Kellie hadn't dressed properly for spending a long period of time in the elements.

"My condo is close by," he said, thinking on his feet. The idea had come to him, and while it appealed strongly, he was unsure how Kellie would feel. "The building is off Cherry Street with a great view of Puget Sound. It's only about a ten-minute, maybe a twelve-minute walk from here. Would you like to head over there, warm up, and share some wine while we wait?"

His spirits rose at her quick nod.

"That sounds lovely."

"Great. I'll get the fireplace going and we'll be warm as toast in only a few minutes."

Her smile was infectious, and he had a hard time looking away.

"That sounds even better."

"I'll check to see if there's any news from my sister," he said, and reached for his phone again.

"Anything?" Kellie asked after he scanned through several texts.

"Not yet." This was unbelievable. In all his years of living in Seattle, not once had he heard about a ferry breaking down and passengers required to wait for hours before being rescued. While it might have been miserable for Avery, he was having a great time.

"I don't understand why they don't simply bring out another ferry and transfer everyone to that instead of all this rigmarole," Kellie said.

Reed understood her frustration. "It isn't that simple. That would be next to impossible with all the vehicles on board. The only solution is to get the repairs done while on the water."

"I feel so bad for those trapped. It's been hours."

"I know; I feel terrible, too." He could only imagine the frustration.

"I mean, it's going to be dark before they arrive," Kellie mentioned, looking up. Dusk had settled over the dimming sky. Within a few minutes it would be completely dark. In the winter months, especially this close to the solstice, night started at around 4:00 or 4:30.

Just then, Reed heard a ping, letting him know he'd received a text. He reached for his phone again and saw that it was from his sister.

Wahoo, the fix is in. If all goes well, we should dock within the next thirty minutes.

Reed shared the text with Kellie.

"At last," she said with a sigh.

"Did you hear anything from your brother?" Avery was far better at sharing updates than Kellie's brother was, he noticed.

"Not yet," she said, glancing down at her phone to be sure.

Tucking Kellie's arm in his elbow, he said, "It looks like this nightmare is about over. Let's head to the ferry terminal."

Kellie's eagerness matched his. They hadn't gone more than a few steps when Kellie paused, slowing her gait. "You mentioned the lunch reservation was for you and your sister, right?"

"Yes." He wasn't sure where this was leading.

"I wonder if your sister was able to get anything to eat on the ferry."

Reed had assumed Avery would have been smart enough to read the situation and buy her lunch. Then again, no one expected the repairs to take as long as they had.

"I don't know if she did or not." Kellie had a good point. He decided to ask Avery. His fingers moved rapidly over the phone keys.

By chance were you able to buy something for lunch? he asked.

Her reply came back within seconds. *No! Everything was sold out before I could. I had a bit of popcorn, but that was it. I'm starving. Hope you have early dinner plans for us.*

Reed shared Avery's response with Kellie.

"I bet my brother didn't have anything to eat, either," she said.

"I didn't make any dinner plans," Reed said. "Did you?"

She shrugged. "Not really. The reason I asked is because I was thinking it would be great, once they arrive, if the four of us went out to eat."

"That would be great, except . . ."

"Except?" she prompted.

"Two things," he said. "We're unlikely to get a reservation so late in the afternoon, especially this close to Christmas. And," he added, "if by some miracle we did, we wouldn't be able to give the restaurant a time."

"Good point," she agreed, sounding discouraged. "I guess we can wait and see how things shake out. I think it would be fun for your sister to meet my brother. Harrison is a terrific guy, and from everything you've said about your sister, I think they'd get along famously."

They continued their walk toward the ferry terminal, their pace slowing as if they realized their fun, adventurous day was about to come to an end. The inside of the terminal was packed with people milling about, most disgruntled by the delays and making their feelings known. A camera crew from a local television station was interviewing those waiting for the stalled ferry. News had spread quickly that the *Yakima* was sure to arrive soon.

Thirty minutes passed before Reed heard someone mention that the disabled ferry wouldn't be arriving anytime soon after all.

He checked his phone and saw that he'd missed a text from Avery.

You won't believe this, Avery wrote. *The engine still isn't working, even after the repair. Everyone is upset. As soon as I know anything, I'll send you word.*

Kellie had her phone in her hand, too, as she'd gotten a text from Harrison. She shared a look with Reed. "It looks like the nightmare will continue."

"What would you like to do?" Reed asked, suggesting a couple options. "We can walk up to my place to wait or remain here."

The madhouse inside the terminal didn't hold any appeal, especially when most everyone was in a cranky mood. It was Kellie's choice, though. He'd stay if it meant he'd be able to spend more time with her.

"Your condo for sure," she said without hesitation. They started to exit when she paused. "We aren't likely to get a dinner reservation, right?"

"Right," he agreed. He hadn't even tried, knowing it was a lost cause.

"Your sister said she was starving, and my guess is that my brother is, too. Let's cook them dinner. We can have it ready by the time they arrive."

Reed loved the idea, although there was a minor complication to her plan. "The problem is all I have for dinner is in the freezer."

Kellie smiled. "Reed, did we not recently walk through the most amazing market filled with everything we would ever want, need, or imagine? How about roasting a salmon filet?"

"The sourdough bread smelled heavenly," he added, favoring the idea.

"And I believe I saw some white asparagus. That would be a real treat."

"Perfect." With a goal in mind, they headed back up the Pike Street Hill Climb to Pike Place Market.

Within ten minutes they had everything they needed. The trip from the market to his condo was a brisk seven-minute walk uphill.

The doorman greeted Reed and sent an appreciative smile at Kellie. "Welcome back, Mr. Bond."

"Thanks, Charley."

"I thought you were collecting your sister? Don't tell me she's one of those unfortunate souls trapped on that Bremerton ferry."

"Unfortunately, she is," he said, as he pushed the button to the elevator.

Reed was having second thoughts as the elevator welcomed them inside, their arms loaded with packages. They'd bought the salmon, found the white asparagus, and added salad fixings and baby potatoes.

Reed enjoyed living in his condo but had never gotten around to adding any homey touches. It was bare bones. He'd gotten a Christmas tree but hadn't taken the time to decorate it, thinking it would be something for him and Avery to do together.

Once inside the door, Kellie paused, looked around, and then smiled.

"I haven't done much decorating," he said self-consciously.

"It's fine, and so *you*."

"So *me*?"

"The brown leather couch with the large-screen television." She motioned to the room he used for his office. "And of course a workstation. The problem is we're both too absorbed in our jobs and other responsibilities. I've lived in my home for three years and there's little more decoration than a few throw pillows on the sofa and a family photo here and there."

"Avery offered to help me," he said as he set the items they'd purchased on the kitchen counter.

They both immediately went to work, standing side by side. He turned on the fireplace and put on some Christmas music. While Kellie prepared the salmon for the oven, he washed the potatoes and, per Kellie's instructions, peeled the asparagus.

Once the fish was ready to roast, Reed opened a bottle of sauvignon blanc he had chilled in the under-counter wine cooler. "Listen, if we get word the ferry is docking, you should stay here where it's warm and cozy. I'll walk down to the terminal to collect Avery and your brother."

She nodded and looked grateful. "You sure you don't mind?"

"Of course. There's no reason for both of us to go out in the cold. Besides, we don't want the fish to overcook."

The only roadblock in his plan would be finding Kellie's brother. He'd need Avery to scout him out before they docked. The solution was simple, if his sister agreed. Reaching for his phone, he called Avery.

She answered almost immediately. "Reed, this waiting is horrible. Everyone is upset and no one knows how much longer this is going to take."

"How are you doing, kiddo?"

"About as well as can be expected. We got word from the captain a few minutes ago that it doesn't look like the ferry can be fixed. He's calling for a tugboat, but no one knows how long that's going to take."

Reed felt awful for Avery and all those who'd been trapped for hours on end.

"If that isn't bad enough, one of the men waiting with us is having a panic attack. Literally. People are helping as best they can. His wife is in labor and at the hospital and he's missing the birth of his first child."

Reed closed his eyes in sympathy.

"On a positive note," Avery added.

His sister always saw the positive side of things.

"His wife isn't on the ferry."

"That's a blessing for sure," Reed said. "I'm sorry you've had such a miserable day. Did I mention earlier that I'd met someone from work, and we spent the afternoon together?" He didn't add that the time with Kellie was one of the most delightful days he'd had in months, not after everything Avery had been through.

"You did, and I'm glad you didn't wait long at the terminal."

"Her brother is on the ferry, and Kellie—that's her name, by the way—was waiting for him at the terminal at the same time I was." Now came the hard part.

"When Kellie learned you hadn't been able to eat lunch, she suggested that the two of us prepare a meal for you and her brother."

"What a thoughtful idea."

He quickly added, knowing what was coming, "The thing is, I need you to connect with her brother."

"Connect? What do you mean?"

"You need to find him, introduce yourself, and explain that I'll be waiting for the two of you at the dock. From there, the three of us will walk to my condo. Kellie will be waiting here."

"Okay, I think."

Avery sounded less enthusiastic now.

"From what she said, her brother is about your age."

The hesitation was longer this time. "Reed," she said, her tone deep and suspicious. "Are you arranging another blind date for me?"

"I knew that was what you'd think," he said quickly, "but I swear this is legit. All you need to do is locate Kellie's brother and tell him the plan."

She huffed a bit. "And how am I supposed to do that?"

Reed hadn't given that part much thought.

"I think it would be a much better idea if Kellie phoned her brother and told him to look for me. You can explain that I'm in the front of the vessel, sitting next to the expectant father."

"But . . ."

"I am not about to go in search of a stranger and tell him that he's joining me for dinner. If Kellie wants me to meet her brother, then she should connect with him and have him find me."

"You're being unreasonable," Reed said, growing irritated.

"I am not going to look for some guy I've never met and invite him to dinner. You're being ridiculous. Let him find me."

"It shouldn't be that hard," he argued.

"I don't mean to be rude," Avery returned with growing impatience. "I'm tired and cranky and the last thing I want to do is play nice with some guy I've never met. All I can think about is getting off this blasted ferry, eating dinner, and then taking a long, hot bubble bath."

Kellie stood close enough to Reed for her to overhear the conversation. "Reed, hold up a minute."

Avery kept arguing, but his attention was on Kellie.

"Avery is right. Harrison should be the one to find her. I'll have him look for her."

Avery's chatter stopped abruptly. "What was that?" she demanded.

"That was Kellie. She said she'd call her brother and have him locate you."

"Yes, yes, I got that part. What did she say his name was?"

"Harrison. Why?"

To his surprise, Avery started to laugh.

"What's so funny?"

"You won't believe this."

"Believe what?"

"Harrison is sitting next to me. We've been talking . . ."

"You mean to say you've already met Harrison? Maybe there's more than one." It seemed too much of a coincidence that his sister and Kellie's brother had found each other all on their own.

"Ask Kellie if her brother is in the Navy and was recently stationed at Bangor?"

Reed didn't need to ask, he already knew the answer. "You've got to be kidding me . . ."

"I'm not," she said, clearly amused.

"Then you won't mind having dinner with me, Kellie, and Harrison?"

She hesitated now. "Harrison is in the Navy, and you know how I feel about . . . Never mind. I'm being ridiculous. Of course I don't object to us joining you and Kellie for dinner."

CHAPTER FOURTEEN

"What was that about?" Harrison asked.

She returned her phone to her purse. "You won't believe this. Our siblings met up at the ferry terminal and spent the day together. As we speak, Kellie is cooking us dinner at my brother's condo."

Harrison appeared as surprised and amazed as Avery was. "You're joking. You mean to say as we were getting to know each other, they were, too?"

"You got it. But listen, this dinner isn't me saying I agree to date you, understand?" She needed to make that clear.

"I'm here, baby, I'm here," James cried out, interrupting the conversation. His grip on the phone was so tight his knuckles had gone pale.

Avery diverted her attention to the expectant father. "What's happening?" she asked, noticing how tense James was. The latest information was that James's neighbor had driven Lilly to the hospital after her water broke.

With a desperation that bordered on panic, he turned to Avery. "I only have five percent battery left on my phone. Do you have a charger?"

"Not with me." She would do whatever she could to help. "Here, take my phone and call your wife with it. Surely someone on board has a charger. I'll find one for you."

"Thank you, thank you."

Speaking to his wife, James said, "Sweetie, hang up and I'll call you back in less than a minute."

Accepting Avery's phone, he gave Avery and Harrison a quick update. "Lilly has been admitted and labor is progressing. As soon as her water broke, her pains increased dramatically. I need to be with her." He looked around frantically, as if by some miracle he could be magically transported to his wife's side.

"Does anyone have an idea when the tugboat will arrive?" he shouted.

The anguish in James's voice seemed to have captured their attention. Travelers in the area gradually stopped talking, the complaints slowly dying down.

A Ferry Merry Christmas 179

Avery overheard people mumbling, asking one another what was happening because clearly James's distress was more than just the impatience and frustration they felt. Curious questions drifted across the open space. A few people moved closer to where James sat, as if to discover what the problem could be.

James was already back on the phone with his wife, so Avery took the opportunity to explain.

Standing on the chair to gather attention, she called out, "James's wife is in labor. It's their first baby."

"Is she alone?"

"Her neighbor was there for a while, but I don't know if she stayed."

James stopped her. "Our neighbor has family obligations and had to leave. All Lilly has for support is me and I'm not there!" he cried out in desperation.

"Tell your wife that we're with her, too," a young woman with an oversized handbag and purple hair shouted out. Looking around her, she said, "Isn't that right?"

Several of those who'd gathered close agreed, with approving nods.

"How far along is her labor?" Beth asked, joining the others. Olivia stood by her side, carefully watching her mother.

"I don't know how far she's dilated," James answered. "Her water broke and she's in the labor room. She said a nurse comes in every now and again to check her."

"Is there anything we can do?" a young woman with heavily tattooed arms asked. She held a knitting project in her lap.

"There is," Avery said. "Does anyone have a charger James can borrow? He's using my phone now, but I only have about forty percent battery left."

"He can use my phone."

"Mine too, if he needs."

A woman in the back stood up. "I have a charger, if he has an iPhone."

Avery saw that he did. "He does." The charger was passed along. Harrison located an outlet and plugged in James's phone.

All at once James started calling out times, looking down at his wrist. "Five seconds. Ten seconds. Twenty. Thirty. Okay. Okay."

A blond woman in a blue cable-knit sweater made her way forward. "My name is Cherise and I'm a nurse. I've worked in labor and delivery. I'll be happy to do what I can to help so you understand the labor process."

James held the phone away from his ear. "Lilly's labor pains are thirty seconds long. Does that mean the baby will be born soon?" His eyes pleaded for any information Cherise had to give him.

"Not necessarily. Is this your first child?"

"Yes." He nodded for emphasis.

"Most likely it will be several hours before your wife delivers."

The relief showed in his shoulders as he relaxed slightly. "That's good. I need to be there for Lilly."

More passengers came closer to where James sat, forming a half-circle around him. When the next labor pain struck and James counted out the seconds, several other voices joined his, loud enough for Lilly to hear.

James looked up and smiled as he explained to his wife what was happening. "Those voices are passengers on the ferry. You aren't alone, Lilly, I'm here and all these people are, too."

The band members Avery had noticed earlier had been some of the loudest complainers about the long delay. They were disgruntled to miss their paying gig and made sure the crew knew about it. It was one of the band members who'd shouted at James earlier when he claimed he needed to get off this ferry. Learning about Lilly, he now seemed regretful.

"We have a singer here!" he shouted out. "Would it help Lilly if we sang to her?"

James asked his wife. "She says it would, especially during the contractions."

"You got it." He called over his shoulder for Tom to retrieve his clarinet. Liam had played his guitar earlier and entertained the children. Olivia had sat front and center, her sweet off-key voice easily distinguishing it from the other kids'.

Once again, James started counting out the seconds, and as before, a loud chorus of voices rose in unison, letting Lilly know she had their support and encouragement.

"The nurse is going to check to see how far Lilly has dilated," James said after this latest contraction. "When she arrived at the hospital, she was at three," James explained. "She hadn't progressed beyond that the last time the nurse checked."

Cherise took the opportunity to explain the three stages of birth to those who were unfamiliar with the terms. "Once Lilly has dilated to ten, the second phase of the birth will start as the baby enters the birth canal."

James held the phone close to his ear and his jaw dropped and he gasped.

"What's happened?" Avery wanted to know.

He blinked several times and then announced, "Lilly is at a seven."

Avery's gaze swiveled to the nurse who stood close to James. Cherise's eyes revealed her surprise. "That's great. Labor is progressing along nicely. How long has it been since Lilly was admitted?"

"Not long," James said. "Maybe thirty or forty minutes." His gaze pleaded with the nurse. "Does that mean I won't make it to the hospital in time for the birth?"

Cherise gestured weakly with her hands. "That remains to be seen."

"Is it a boy or a girl?" the woman with the tattoos on her arms asked.

James pushed the hair away from his forehead. "We don't know. We chose to wait. We just want a healthy baby."

"A Christmas surprise."

James jerked and straightened. "Lilly's having another contraction."

It seemed like everyone on the entire deck helped count out the forty-five seconds.

Once again, James looked to the nurse, eager for any information. "That's ten seconds longer than the last contraction," he announced, as if this earth-shattering information required an explanation.

"It was," Cherise agreed, without adding anything else.

If James was hoping for some medical insight, he was disappointed.

Avery heard Lilly's faint voice, since she was the one sitting closest to James. He listened and smiled.

Holding the phone away from his ear, James looked up and said, "Lilly wants you all to know that she appreciates the support. She can hear you, and it's helping her deal with the pain."

A couple folks exchanged high fives.

"We took birthing classes when Lilly was six months along. Lilly wanted to give birth naturally, but it was understood I'd be right beside her. She says with all of us helping, she doesn't feel alone and is better able to manage the birth right now without the epidural."

A cheer of support followed.

Tom started strumming his guitar. "Liam and Suzie, what should we play?"

"What kind of music does your wife enjoy?" Liam asked.

"Country," James answered. "New country—you know, like Jelly Roll or Lainey Wilson."

"Got it," Liam said, as he took a seat and rested his guitar on his thigh. "Let us know when the next contraction starts, and Suzie and I will start singing. I hope it helps."

"Now!" James shouted a few minutes later, holding

the phone out toward Liam and the tall woman standing at his side to better pick up the music.

Liam and Tom immediately started playing, with Suzie's alto voice blending in beautifully. It took Avery less than a second to recognize the classic "Fast Car." It sounded almost as if Tracy Chapman and Luke Combs were singing the duet.

While they sang, those close by started counting out the seconds, along with James. They must have caused something of a ruckus because Earl Jones and another crewman appeared.

"What's going on up here?" Earl demanded, scrutinizing the way nearly everyone on the passenger deck had gathered around James.

Before anyone was able to answer, he figured it out himself. "You mean the guy with the pregnant wife is the cause of all this?"

Avery nodded. "Her water broke right after the speedboat left and she's in the labor room by herself. We're all trying to help her feel less alone."

Earl did a quick study of the situation and stood, amazed when Lilly had another contraction. Liam and Suzie broke into a country-style Christmas song next while everyone else counted down the seconds. Avery didn't recognize the lyrics but could tell the singing was helping Lilly and James, too.

"I've got a Bluetooth speaker," the second crewman offered. "That way everyone can hear Lilly, if she'd like that."

James asked his wife. "Lilly said she'd love that."

The crewman left and returned no more than a minute later. It took even less time than that to connect the phone with his speaker.

Once it was operational, Cherise encouraged Lilly. "Lilly, rest as best you can between contractions. Take in deep breaths and let them out slowly."

"Did you hear that, sweetie?" James asked.

"I did. Can everyone hear me okay?"

James looked up and saw several people nodding. "They can." She must have said something more, something Avery wasn't able to hear.

James relaxed. "Lilly wants everyone to know how much the counting helps."

"We're happy to be here," Virginia assured her.

Another contraction was serenaded by the two band members. Other voices joined in while those counting the seconds added to the cacophony.

Watching the crowd, it came to Avery that before helping Lilly everyone had been varying degrees of annoyed and angry after the news regarding the failed engine part. The entire atmosphere had now shifted while helping James and Lilly.

The grumbling had all but disappeared. Only a few minutes earlier, James had been understandably distraught and tense. He seemed much calmer now. What had felt like a disaster earlier had brought them all together, given them a purpose.

Beth and Olivia stood side by side. Every now and again Beth would bend closer to her daughter. Avery guessed it was to explain to the little girl what was taking place and why everyone was gathered around James.

From the far side of the room, she noticed the man Olivia had identified as her father come to stand beside Beth and Olivia. He glanced at his wife and seemed to want her attention. Only Beth refused to look at him.

Avery couldn't help but wonder what all that was about.

CHAPTER FIFTEEN

Beth ignored Logan even though he'd positioned himself so that he stood next to her and Olivia. He'd bruised her heart—and more important, Olivia's—with his decision to bow out of Christmas. Yet, as hard as she tried, she could feel herself drawn to him, drawn into the memories of the love they'd once shared. For months on end, she'd prayed and hoped that eventually Logan would realize he'd made a mistake and return home.

Her love for him and all the might-have-beens made her weak. For so long after Logan left, she'd believed he'd realize he belonged with his wife and daughter and would come back to them. Four months passed before she found the courage to tell her parents Logan had moved out. Until that time, she'd invented excuses for why he wasn't around.

He was working overtime.

He was at a friend's house, watching a Seahawks football game.

He was out running errands.

The sad part was that her parents believed her. Beth was forced to admit the truth to her family when it became *her* truth. Logan wasn't going to change his mind. He'd made his decision and had no intention of being part of their family any longer. She knew her parents would loan her the money to file for a divorce. At any point, she could have taken advantage of their generosity. Only Beth couldn't make herself give up the hope that one day they would be willing to open up to each other and communicate, talking through their issues together.

"I couldn't do it," Logan said, breaking into her thoughts.

Beth ignored him.

James's wife was having another contraction, and with the crowd gathered around the young man, Beth and Olivia started counting out the seconds.

When the counting and the singing ceased, Logan said it again, a bit louder this time. "I couldn't do it."

Seeing that he wasn't going to let her pretend she hadn't heard him, she turned her head just enough to look at him. "Do what?"

He lowered his head. "Tell Olivia I wouldn't be there for Christmas."

Unsure of what he expected her to say or what she should feel, she decided it was best to say nothing.

"She was so happy when she thought I'd be with the two of you," he continued. "I can't disappoint her."

When he'd told her he'd changed his mind, she'd wanted to shout at him, calling him a coward. If they had been anywhere but on a crowded ferry, she would have said what was on her mind.

The truth, the bottom line, was that Logan was afraid of facing her parents, knowing they were helping her not only with Olivia's medical bills but also with other expenses.

Beth knew he feared her mom or dad would call him out for the way he'd given up on them and mostly on himself. Rather than face the possibility, he'd chosen to crush Olivia's joy.

"You mean to say you'll be joining us?" she asked.

He didn't look the least bit enthused. "I'll come for a little while . . . I don't have any gifts for anyone; I won't stay long."

"Okay," she said.

He stuffed his hands into his pockets. "I'm sorry, I'd hoped to have something for you and Olivia."

"We don't need gifts," she said, struggling to keep her voice even. Olivia and Beth wanted nothing more than for him to come home so they could be a family again.

"More than life itself, I wish I could have been the man you believed I could be," he continued in low tones. "I tried, Beth. I sincerely tried. Everything I did turned out wrong."

She jerked her head back around to stare at him. "Everything you did showed that you cared, that even when money was tight, we still had each other and Olivia. We used to be a team, Logan, working together to build a family. Yes, there were problems, bills, stress, budget shortfalls. But we had each other until you left me to stand alone with a broken heart. I know how wrong it was for me to take that money from Mom and Dad without telling you, but . . ." Her voice cracked and she swallowed down a sob, angry with herself for letting him see her pain.

This was the first real conversation they'd had about his leaving. At first, after he'd left, she'd been too shocked to react, certain he would quickly change his mind and move back. Every conversation had been one she hoped would bring him home. Words he apparently didn't want to hear because he'd stopped having more than a brief conversation when he collected Olivia, as if he couldn't get away fast enough.

For far longer than she should have, Beth clung to the hope that Logan would change his mind. When it seemed that wasn't going to happen, she broke down and wept bitter tears, refusing to beg, refusing to accept that he no longer wanted to be part of their lives.

Her hope had been replaced with heartache and despair. Because of his background, she realized how hard Logan struggled with his self-esteem. His father had beaten him down to the point where he struggled to make himself believe he was capable of becoming a success in life.

By the time a year passed, she became angry and bitter, but soon she realized how pointless resentment was. For a long while she struggled with acceptance and concentrated on being the best mom, daughter, and teacher that she could be. She had to let go and give Logan to God and pray that one day he'd come to accept how much he was loved.

"I'm sorry," he repeated.

Tears were close to the surface, and once again her voice wobbled when she spoke. "I know." Although it was tearing her up inside, she had to find the strength within herself to be grateful for whatever Logan was able to give of himself. If not for her, then for Olivia's sake.

Once she felt she could keep her voice even, she said, "Having you spend even a short time with Olivia on Christmas will mean everything to her."

"Like I said, I . . . I don't have a gift for her," he said. "I was hoping to sell my motorcycle, but the buyer changed his mind at the last minute." Disappointment coated each word.

Beth remembered how still he'd gotten after reading a message on his phone. It was shortly after that when he'd decided to forgo Christmas with them.

"I'm glad he changed his mind. You love that bike."

"I love Olivia more and was hoping to get her a Christmas gift . . . and you, too."

Her lower lip quivered as she fought back emotion. That Logan would be willing to sacrifice his bike to give them Christmas gifts was like a punch to the heart. As hard as he pretended not to care, he clearly did.

Reaching for his hand, Beth entwined her fingers with his. It was all she could do without tearing up to reveal how deeply his words had touched her.

The singing and counting started up again, and this time Logan joined in, his voice blending in with Beth's.

"That man's wife is having a baby," Olivia explained,

coming to stand on the other side of Logan. He reached for his daughter's hand and smiled down at her.

"The daddy can't be with his wife because he's stuck on the ferry like us," Olivia added, as if this was news to Logan.

"That's why we're all helping him and his wife, too," Beth explained.

"Daddy." Olivia looked up at Logan, her beautiful brown eyes so like her father's, and asked, "Was I born in a hospital?"

"Yup, you sure were."

"Were you there with Mommy?"

"I was."

"Did you count the seconds of the contraptions like everyone is doing here?"

"Contractions," Beth corrected.

"Con-trac-tions," Olivia repeated, struggling to pronounce the multisyllable word.

Logan nodded. "I did. I was right by your mommy's side the whole time."

"Was Mommy in pain, like the lady?"

Olivia had grown more inquisitive as she listened to the conversations taking place around them. "I was," Beth said, "but it was the best pain in the world because when it was over I got to hold you in my arms."

Olivia cocked her head to one side as if she found

Beth's answer hard to understand. "When I get hurt and you kiss my owie, it sometimes feels better and sometimes it still hurts."

"A little attention and love make almost all the pain go away," Beth said.

"Yup, it does." Olivia's attention waned and she asked, "Can I go sit with my new friend?"

"Okay," Beth agreed.

Her daughter skipped happily to the table where Kevin sat coloring in a book. The boy glanced up and smiled when Olivia approached. Soon the two sat side by side, each coloring a page. Sharing crayons.

"I remember when you went into labor," Logan said, as he glanced down at their clasped hands. "I was scared to death."

"You were?" All she remembered was how calm he was, how caring and thoughtful. "You certainly didn't show it."

"I didn't dare. I was afraid if you knew how frightened I was you would panic yourself."

"I think I probably would have," Beth agreed, remembering the hectic drive to the hospital after they realized the strange pain she was experiencing that emanated from her back was the first sign of labor. "It was too early, and I didn't know what that would mean for the baby."

A loud cheer went up. Because of the conversation with Logan, Beth hadn't been paying attention to what was going on around them.

She touched Virginia's shoulder, as she was standing in front of Beth.

"Did something just happen?"

The grandmother turned her head around. "Lilly has advanced to stage two—the baby is about to be born."

"So soon?"

"A fast labor for sure, and it's their first," Virginia said and smiled. "I wasn't that fortunate with either of my two children."

"I wasn't, either," Beth said as the two women shared a smile. When she returned her attention to Logan, she noticed how intently he was staring at her.

"Is everything all right?" she asked, wondering at the change in him.

He looked away, and Beth thought she might have seen the sheen of tears in his eyes.

"Logan? What is it?"

He didn't answer for a moment. "When Olivia was born, I was terrified I would lose you both."

All Beth remembered was how concerned she was for her baby. As labor progressed, problems arose. Two doctors and a nurse fussed around her. The pains were strong and depleted her energy. She'd closed her eyes and concentrated on dealing with the pain and freeing this new life from her body.

"The doctors told me Olivia was in distress," Logan said. "I didn't know what that meant and no one took the time to explain what was happening. All the doctor told me was that they needed to help you deliver the baby as quickly as possible."

Beth had been aware of the difficulties with Olivia's lungs following her birth, but not right away. Her head had been pounding with a dull ache and it felt as if she grew weaker with each contraction.

"Olivia didn't cry when she was born," Logan reminded her.

"Yes . . . I remember that. Her lack of response was due to her lung development."

"She was born blue, Beth, completely blue, and her chest had caved in and . . . you were completely out of it."

Beth had contracted an infection. Whether it came from home or in the hospital they would never know. The night of Olivia's birth, Beth's fever spiked to 105 degrees.

"The doctors rushed Olivia out of the room," Logan continued. "I was afraid to leave you, but I needed to know what was wrong with our daughter. They placed her in the NICU and hooked her tiny body up to oxygen. I thank God you weren't there to see me. I fell apart and started crying, terrified I was about to lose both my wife and my baby."

Beth knew none of this. "I had no idea."

"How could you? By the time I was able to get back to you, they had you hooked up to antibiotics. The nursing staff was doing everything possible to bring down your fever.

"I sat by your bedside all night, praying and begging God to not take you from me. The nurse tried to make me leave, but I refused. I caused enough of a stir that they let me stay."

"You were with me all night?" Exhausted as she'd been, Beth had slept for nearly ten hours.

"I went back and forth between you and Olivia."

"I remember you were in the room when I woke." Her fever had remained high. Much of the time after Olivia's birth remained hazy.

"The first thing you asked me was about Olivia. I was afraid to tell you how close we came to losing her. Thankfully, you were sleeping during the worst of it."

Beth smiled. "Our baby girl is a fighter."

Logan's eyes grew warm, and a soft smile touched the edges of his mouth. "The first time I was able to touch her, she reached for my finger. I didn't know what to expect, what being a father would mean. As I watched her chest rise and fall, I knew there was nothing I wouldn't do to keep her safe. I'm not much of a praying man, yet in that moment I begged God to let her live.

"I wish I could explain this intense feeling that came over me in that moment. There was this pull, this tug on my heart. It was physical. I placed my hand there because I was half afraid I was having some kind of seizure. I couldn't believe the strength of it as I stared down at this tiny life we'd created. In that moment I knew I would love this child more than anything." His eyes shone with the sincerity of his words.

Beth wiped away a stray tear as it meandered down her cheek. Leaning her head toward Logan, she rested against his shoulder.

"I could never love you more than I did the night Olivia was born. You were so brave and strong. I've never deserved you, Beth. I desperately wanted to be a good provider and husband and I failed on all fronts."

"You didn't fail me, Logan," she whispered.

"I did," he insisted. "When I learned your parents were helping with the medical bills, I felt like less than a man that I couldn't care for my family properly."

Knowing how proud Logan was, Beth blamed herself. "I should have told you. Keeping it a secret was a betrayal that only added to your fears about caring for your family."

"Telling me or not wouldn't have made a difference. I couldn't support my family and so, right or wrong, I left."

Beth shifted her position until she stood directly in front of Logan. "Tell me, Logan, and please be honest. Do you regret leaving Olivia and me?"

For the longest moment, he didn't answer. When he finally did, his voice was low and full of emotion. "Every single day."

"Then why . . . ?"

"I thought you'd meet someone else, someone who could give you the things you and Olivia deserve."

Beth felt like laughing and crying both at once. "I don't want anyone else. You're the one I love. You're the one Olivia adores. Come back to us, Logan. We love and need you more than any gift you can give, more than anything else this world has to offer." Her hands framed his face. "I love you. I always have and I always will. The only man I want in my life is you."

Tears ran freely down his cheeks. "Do you really mean it? You'd take me back after everything I've done to mess up our family?"

"It would be the best Christmas of my life if you agreed."

He swallowed tightly and then wrapped Beth in his arms and squeezed her so close and tight that she could barely manage to breathe.

"I don't deserve you and Olivia," he argued.

"No, you don't, but you have us anyway, and we're never letting you leave us again. Got it?"

"Got it," he repeated.

A loud cheer arose, and Beth noticed people exchanging high fives. She looked at Logan. His arms remained around her, holding her close.

"My guess is we have a Christmas baby."

CHAPTER SIXTEEN

The moment was intense. James's wife, Lilly, was delivering the baby. James had his head bowed and seemed to be praying. All of a sudden, the weak cry of an infant sounded over the Bluetooth speaker and the room erupted into joyous laughter and hoots of delight.

James jerked his head up. With the phone to his ear, he asked, "Is the baby a boy or a girl?"

The doctor's voice boomed over the speaker. "You have a beautiful baby girl."

James leaped to his feet, his face bright with tears. "Did you hear?" he shouted to anyone and everyone who would listen. "I have a daughter." Tossing his arms into the air, he danced around in a circle, stamping his feet.

The young father wasn't the only one caught up in the happy excitement. Several couples joined hands and skipped around in circles as if they themselves had been the happy recipients of a new son or daughter. Others exchanged high fives, and several clapped James's shoulder to the point where he nearly stumbled forward. Little could distract from the joyful emotion that filled James's expression. He hadn't been at Lilly's side when she delivered their daughter, but he had a group of strangers who stood by him and Lilly with support and encouragement, sharing this moment. Avery found it hard to believe the total transformation that had taken place after the replacement part didn't repair the engine. None of those disappointments seemed to matter. A baby had been born and each one who stood at James's side shared in the wonder and the miracle of it.

Harrison was next to her, and she smiled up at him, enjoying the revelry taking place around them. She was grateful to have played a small role in helping James and his wife.

Harrison slipped his arm around her waist. "This is crazy," he whispered close to her ear so she could hear him above all the racket.

"It's a good kind of crazy, though," she said, and laughed when a man broke into a beatboxing dance. A small group formed around him with people clapping.

A Ferry Merry Christmas 205

For many, the hours they'd been forced to wait had been a trial. Avery had spent the majority of the time getting to know Harrison, afraid she would succumb to his charm. It became a constant battle of wills, all within herself. She'd agreed to give him a chance, and at the time it had seemed fair. But she'd assumed it would be only the time it took to sail from Bremerton to Seattle, not this prolonged wait. She'd spent the time talking to Harrison and him with her. They'd found a common goal in helping James.

To his credit, Harrison had used the time effectively, sharing himself with her, telling her about his dreams, his desire to serve the country with his work in the Navy. Avery had listened and found him easy to be with. Too easy. He asked about her life and appeared genuinely interested. She knew that at the end of the day, he would want his answer.

Now here they were, caught up in this celebration, and she couldn't keep from smiling up at him, her heart exposed, staring deep into his eyes.

"I know you haven't agreed to see me beyond today, but I'm hoping you'll be willing to give me a chance."

"I . . ." She didn't know what to tell him. "We'll be having dinner together later with our siblings. Let's not get caught up in the emotions of the moment. I think it would be best to give us each a few days to think this through."

"Then you'll agree to see me again after Christmas?"

She nodded. "I will." This moment of joy made it far too easy to give in to what her heart was telling her. Agreeing to date Harrison was what she wanted, but her mind and heart were cautious. She didn't want to get caught up in the excitement and regret it later.

"I'm willing to wait," he agreed, with some reluctance. "However, before we step off this ferry, I'd very much like to kiss you."

Avery's heart had no objection whatsoever. She didn't even try to talk herself out of it. Slipping her arms over his shoulders, she knotted her hands behind his neck. "I think that's a reasonable request."

Harrison lowered his mouth to hers as his arms tightened around her waist, half lifting her off the floor. His kiss was tender, gentle, sweet, and ever so welcome. When he released her, his gaze held hers.

"You know how I feel, and I hope you're feeling the same."

"I do," she admitted, her heart racing. "I do."

"I don't have a girl in every port, Avery. As a submariner, the only women I'm likely to meet are mermaids."

She smiled at his joke.

"I'm sorry you were hurt before, but I'm willing to

give you those few days because you're worth it. I want to see you again," Harrison said. "A day or two after Christmas," he repeated and exhaled a slow breath. "I'll be as patient as I can be, but please don't leave me hanging."

Earl Jones sauntered in, and with hands on his hips looked around at the chaos taking place. Studying the craziness going on around the passenger deck, he slowly shook his head. When no one seemed to notice his arrival, he whistled and raised his arms to get everyone's attention.

"While you yahoos were up here making all kinds of racket, no one seemed to notice the tugboat has arrived. We'll be docking within the next thirty minutes."

A loud cheer arose.

"Unless something else happens," Harrison's friend Kyle jokingly suggested.

"Nothing else is going to delay us," Earl assured him as he headed toward the stairwell.

"I have a daughter," James called out, stopping Earl in his tracks at the good news. "Me. A daughter. I have a little girl. We're naming her Noelle Rose."

"Congratulations." Earl's smile was wide and genuine. "I've got a daughter myself. Watch out, baby girls have a way of wrapping us around their little fingers."

"Everyone has been so great," James told him. "This has been the best day of my life."

Virginia smiled down at Olivia. "Isn't this the most glorious news?"

Olivia nodded eagerly.

"It's the kind of news that calls for a celebration. Actually, I have one of my own."

"You do?" Avery asked, then remembered the tin of cookies Virginia had shared, wondering if those baked goods were meant for something or someone else.

A peaceful look stole over the other woman. "My sister and I had a falling-out a few years back. Those cookies were a special family recipe handed down from our mother. It's only fitting that those gingerbread men would be the means of reuniting me with my twin."

"But you gave them away," Avery said, not realizing what a sacrifice it had been on the other woman's part.

"Veronica won't mind. We both know the cookies were simply an excuse to reach out and facilitate our reconciliation. It was something we both wanted, with or without the cookies."

"Making up with your twin is the celebration you mentioned, then?"

"Yes, and now with the baby it feels like even more of one."

"You're right, Grandma," Liam said. He'd apparently overheard their conversation. "This is a great time to celebrate. Come on, guys, we aren't going to make it to the wedding, but we can still entertain."

The other members of the band quickly retrieved their instruments from the car deck. The band set up in front of the ferry. Olivia and Kevin, her newfound friend, stood in the very front, shaking with excitement, eager to continue the songfest, and this time with the entire band playing.

"Can you play 'Frosty the Snowman'?" Olivia shouted.

"'Grandma Got Run Over by a Reindeer'?" Kevin called out next.

Liam and his friends exchanged glances. "We sure can!"

The keyboard player started the tune, and the other instruments quickly joined in. Olivia and a couple other children started singing, which was all the encouragement the adults needed. Soon the deck echoed with the sounds of their blended voices. The few children who stood together clapped their hands with glee and danced around the deck.

"Grandma Got Run Over by a Reindeer" was followed by the Brenda Lee hit from years ago that had experienced a recent revival, "Rocking Around the Christmas Tree." A few started their own rocking, swing-dancing and showing off their fancy footwork.

The singing was boisterous and full of good cheer. Standing toward the back of the crowd, Avery watched what was happening with amusement. Everything had changed for the better. The mood in the room got an additional emotional boost after everyone learned they were about to be rescued.

Before she could fully take in what was happening, a conga line had formed. A string of merrymakers danced their way around the entire area, kicking, singing, laughing.

"Come on," Harrison said, as he reached for Avery's hand.

Laughing, she joined him at the end of the line.

As they circled the deck, Avery noticed Olivia standing on a chair clapping her hands, her sweet face glowing with joy. When she noticed Avery, she jumped down and ran over to her.

Avery and Harrison stepped out of the line to see what the youngster had to say that was so important.

"Guess what?" she shouted, and then answered her own question. "Daddy is going to come live with me and Mommy again."

Avery had wondered. She'd seen the two adults talking with their heads leaning toward each other. Earlier, Oliva's dad sat at the table in the small cafeteria and slumped forward as if he carried the weight of the world on his shoulders. Clearly something had taken place that had put matters straight.

"That's wonderful," she told Olivia, who was beaming with happiness knowing she would be with her mommy and daddy for Christmas.

"It's the best news ever," Olivia said, and with that, she raced back to where she'd been standing and continued clapping.

Avery considered this news one of the many Christmas miracles she'd witnessed that day. A baby's birth. A chance meeting. Hearts healed. She suspected there were more she knew nothing about.

As she watched Olivia, she felt a slight shift on the deck that caused her to take a single step forward.

The ferry was moving.

To be sure, she went to look out the window. The city lights came into view, bright and welcoming. All afternoon she'd waited patiently to see this very sight. Oddly, she felt a strange sense of disappointment. Their adventure was about to end just when it felt like everything had righted itself.

Harrison came to stand behind her. "It won't be long now," he said, his hand resting on the small of her back.

Looking over her shoulder, she commented, "As ridiculous as it sounds, I'm almost sorry to be leaving."

"I know. I was thinking the same thing."

"Look," she said, pointing to the tugboat, which had positioned itself against the side of the ferry. It was decorated with strings of multicolored lights as it nudged the huge vessel toward the dock.

They were soon joined by others and the band broke into "Auld Lang Syne," which sent a wave of laughter through the deck.

It wasn't long before they reached the dock. Cheers rose, along with applause that after the extended wait, they had finally reached their destination.

Soon passengers started to gather their belongings. Those who'd driven on returned to the car deck while the walk-ons stood by the door leading to the exit ramp. When boarding the ferry in Bremerton, there had been a rush as people jockeyed for seats. Unusual as it seemed, no one appeared to feel that same sense of urgency now.

Avery supposed it had to do with the camaraderie while stranded. A common purpose that had brought them together. Hearing the first cries of a new life coming into the world had changed them. Had changed Avery.

James came to stand by her and Harrison. "I wanted to thank you," he said, his expression radiant. "I don't know what I would have done if you hadn't been willing to lend me your phone."

"It was nothing," Avery assured him.

"It was everything," he countered. "I'll be heading directly to the hospital, but before I leave, I wanted to give you my business card." He handed her his card. "I'd like to send you a photo of Noelle, if you don't mind."

"Mind?" she countered. "I'd be thrilled."

"She weighed seven pounds, four ounces, and is twenty inches long. Lilly thinks she's going to be tall like her daddy."

He started toward the end of the line, which parted like the Red Sea, as if he were Moses holding a staff. Logan had lingered on deck with his wife and daughter. When he saw James, he moved forward and offered him a ride on his motorcycle to the hospital.

As James left with Logan, people slapped his back and congratulated him again.

"Are you ready?" Harrison asked.

"Sure thing," Avery said. "My brother sent a text. He's waiting for us at the end of the ramp."

Harrison reached for her hand, and together they headed toward the exit.

CHAPTER SEVENTEEN

Virginia stepped off the ferry and walked into the crowded terminal. It was difficult to maneuver as people surged forward to greet those who had been trapped on the ferry.

What an adventure this trip had been, beginning to end. To share even a small part in the birth of James's daughter had made Virginia's heart sing. New life did that, inspiring hope and joy. Watching James's tears when he first heard his daughter's cry had brought tears to her own eyes.

Stepping aside, Virginia let others move ahead of her. She would need to find an Uber and she wasn't sure how long that would take. Before she left the ferry she sent Veronica a text, letting her know she should arrive soon, if it wasn't too late to visit.

Veronica had immediately sent a text back.

You're welcome any time you arrive.

A warm feeling had come over her with the hope that the two of them would be able to put the past behind them and move forward.

Feeling she should remind Veronica that she'd given away the cookies, she sent a second text.

Oh, and we helped deliver a baby. Long story. I can't wait to tell you all about it.

Veronica texted back.

Baby? You helped deliver a baby? Never mind, you can tell me later.

Virginia watched as Avery and Harrison were met by a young man. He hugged Avery and shook hands with Harrison. Noticing Virginia, Avery held out her hand.

"Virginia, come meet my brother."

Brother and sister stood side by side. The family resemblance was hard to miss. They shared the same brown eyes and high foreheads and engaging smiles.

"This is Reed," Avery said.

She went on to give Virginia a brief telling of how she'd met Harrison and Reed had stumbled upon Harrison's sister while waiting inside the terminal. The coincidence was fun and caused her imagination to run. It seemed a lot had happened in the hours they'd been stalled on the water.

"Virginia was generous enough to share her mother's holiday cookies with everyone," Avery told her brother. "You can't imagine how beautifully decorated they were."

"And tasty," Harrison added.

She blushed at their praise.

"Nice meeting you, Virginia," Reed said as he steered them toward the exit. "Kellie has dinner waiting at the condo."

"Merry Christmas," Virginia said as they headed outside.

Bundling her scarf around her neck to ward off the cold, Virginia headed out of the terminal building and into the dark. As expected, the cold hit her like a slap in the face and she sucked in a deep breath. The sidewalk in front of the building was jammed with those seeking transportation. There was nothing for Virginia to do but wait her turn.

A voice caught her attention. For a moment she thought she heard someone call her name. Glancing around, she didn't see or hear anything more and was convinced she'd imagined it.

Then her name came again, closer this time.

Certain now that someone had indeed called for her,

Virginia turned around, seeking out whoever it might be. It wasn't a voice she recognized.

A young woman came rushing toward her, relief showing on her face. "Aunt Virginia?"

Virginia blinked. It couldn't be, could it? This must be her grandniece, whom she hadn't seen in several years.

"Phoebe?" My goodness, the young teen she remembered was a strikingly beautiful young woman now.

"Grandma sent us to collect you. My boyfriend is double-parked just down the street." She took hold of Virginia's arm and hurriedly led her toward the car.

Once inside the vehicle, Virginia relaxed against the back of the seat. "Oh my, I wish I'd known to expect you."

"Didn't Grandma send you a text?"

Feeling guilty, Virginia grabbed her phone and realized Veronica had indeed let her know Phoebe would pick her up at the ferry dock. "She did. I didn't see it, though. Sorry."

"No worries, I found you. Mom and Grandma can't wait to see you."

Virginia felt much the same when it came to this visit with her twin and her grandniece.

The ride took fifteen minutes in the traffic. Phoebe's boyfriend parked in front of the house. No sooner had

A Ferry Merry Christmas

he turned off the engine when the front door opened and Veronica stepped onto the porch.

Virginia climbed out of the car and tears filled her eyes. Her sister was eager to see her, eager to put the past behind them. Eager to share the closeness they'd once had and lost. It felt like a Christmas miracle.

They met halfway to the house and embraced. Veronica had tears in her eyes, too. "You can have Mom's pearls," she whispered, hugging Virigina tightly around the waist. "The only reason I wanted them was because I knew you did. It was unforgivable of me, and I'm so sorry."

"You can have the china," Virginia said, fresh tears raining down her cheeks. "It was selfish of me to take it knowing how much you treasured that set. I haven't used it even once. It's all yours."

With their arms around each other's waists, they walked into the house.

Sniffling, Veronica said, "Now tell me about this baby."

And so Virginia did, not omitting a single detail.

CHAPTER EIGHTEEN

A great deal had happened between the time the ferry reached Seattle and Christmas Day for Beth and Logan. Olivia had her chance to see Santa with her parents at her side. For the first time since Logan had decided to move out, they'd talked. Really talked, baring their souls to each other. Even after reconciling, Beth knew Logan was nervous about spending Christmas Day with her family.

Logan admitted that his pride had gotten in the way of doing what was best for his family. Learning that Beth's parents had pitched in to ease the financial burden following Olivia's birth had made him feel like less of a man. For reasons she couldn't fully understand, he felt that he had failed in his responsibilities.

Beth willingly admitted her own part in the breakup of their marriage. She should never have hidden her family's participation in paying off their debts. She'd meant well, but it had backfired on her and wounded her husband. Then, instead of dealing with the issue, she'd done her best to pretend everything was fine when it clearly wasn't. If only they'd been able to talk earlier, then these two years of misery might have been avoided.

The contrast between the way he'd grown up and Beth's childhood was striking. His father was an alcoholic and his mother had run off when he was a teenager. Logan hadn't talked to either of them in years.

As a result, he'd never been completely comfortable around her close-knit family when his own had been so completely dysfunctional. Hard as her parents and siblings tried, Logan found it difficult to fit in.

It went without saying how much he loved Beth and adored their daughter. However, being part of a real family had overwhelmed him. He admitted he never understood what Beth saw in him. He'd never been unconditionally loved and accepted, and he struggled with finding his place in the fold.

At family functions, he was prone to sit back and watch, although he had to admit he enjoyed himself.

They parked in front of Beth's family home. Beth noticed that Logan's hands remained on the steering wheel, as if he were afraid to let go.

"It's going to be fine," she assured him, gently placing her hand on his forearm.

His nod was weak. "It's been a while since I've seen your parents, and I guess I'm worried that we're all going to be uncomfortable. Should I mention it? Or would it be best to say nothing?"

Beth's brow creased as she considered his question. "Play it by ear. My thought is that if anyone questions you leaving, it will be my dad. For Mom's part, I think she's pleased we've reconciled for Olivia's sake, knowing how much our daughter loves her daddy."

"I'd hoped to bring your parents a gift . . ."

"Logan," Beth said reassuringly, her hand tightening over his forearm. "You're giving my parents the best possible gift they could ever want."

He turned to face her, his eyes full of doubt.

"You're gifting my parents with a happy daughter and granddaughter."

"Daddy," Olivia said from the back seat. "Are you going to live with us forever and ever?"

Even now Olivia needed to be reassured that her daddy wouldn't leave them again.

Logan relaxed. "Yes, pumpkin."

"That's my best Christmas present ever. And next year, I want you and Mommy to give me a little sister."

The blood drained from Logan's face, and he chuckled.

"All in good time," Beth told her daughter, smiling herself.

Logan reached for her hand and gave it a squeeze. "I'd like that, too."

"Me, too," Beth said, nearly bursting with all the love she felt for her husband.

While Logan helped Olivia out of the rear seat, Beth collected the sweet-potato dish. It was a family favorite and something she could contribute for their dinner. Josie, her younger sister, who was home from college, threw open the front door and raced down the sidewalk to greet them. Keith, Beth's older brother, was spending Christmas with his wife's family.

"Aunt Josie, Aunt Josie, Santa brought me an iPad and socks and a Christmas dress. See?" Olivia whirled around, the bright red skirt flaring out as she turned two full circles. "Isn't it pretty?"

"It's beautiful and so are you."

"I know," Olivia said, as if it were a well-known fact. "My daddy tells me that all the time."

Beth's sister laughed and hugged Olivia. Taking

hold of Olivia's hand, she smiled at Logan. "Good to see you, Logan. Merry Christmas."

From the warmth of her sister's greeting, some of the stress seemed to leave his shoulders.

Logan stood beside Beth. "I'll carry that," he said, removing the casserole dish from her hands. Olivia and Josie were already inside the house. When Beth arrived, Olivia was entertaining her grandpa, showing off her Christmas dress, dancing around like she was part of a ballet.

Beth followed Logan into the kitchen, where her mother was busy preparing dinner.

Her mother's eyes lit up when she saw Logan.

"Where would you like this?" he asked, already feeling uncomfortable.

Her mother dried her hands on her apron and pointed to the counter. "Set it over there. How long does it need to be in the oven?"

"Thirty minutes," Beth supplied. "At 350."

"Got it." She walked over to Logan. "It's good to see you, Logan."

And then, to his surprise, she opened her arms wide and hugged him tightly. "I hope you know you broke our daughter's heart," she whispered in his ear.

Logan swallowed hard and nodded. "I do, and I have no intention of doing it again."

"Then we're good," Irene said, and released him.

Logan nodded and swallowed tightly, his eyes full of emotion. "Thank you for agreeing to let me come for Christmas," he said, and his voice grew hoarse with emotion.

"No need to thank us," she continued. "You're family."

Family. He had a family, a real one, with love and acceptance. He'd been a fool to turn his back on the very thing he most craved.

"Dinner will be ready soon," Irene said, as she returned to cutting the fresh fruit for the salad.

"What can I do to help?" Beth asked.

Logan left the women in the kitchen and wandered into the family room, where Grant, Beth's father, was being entertained by Olivia.

A football game played on the television, and not knowing what else to do, Logan sat in the chair next to Grant. When Logan first met Beth's family, he'd half expected them to tell their daughter she could do better. Likely the only reason they didn't was because it was clear how deeply he loved Beth. God knew he was crazy about her. Then and now. Even more so now.

They'd met when he signed up for a night class in marketing. He first saw Beth in the school library and couldn't take his eyes off her. It took three weeks before he found the courage to ask her out for coffee. It stunned him when she agreed.

That night they'd talked for hours. Soon they met after class, and she helped him study. When he passed both courses with high grades, she'd thrown her arms around him, and they kissed. Logan thought he'd gone to heaven, he was so in love with this vivacious, beautiful woman.

When Beth brought him home to meet her family, he hadn't known what to expect. Certainly not this easy acceptance. Even with all the odds stacked against him, Grant and Irene had welcomed him with as much enthusiasm as they would have a trust-fund baby.

Logan saw Beth every day that summer. When she returned for her last year of college, he was convinced she'd forget all about him. It made no sense that she'd stick with him when she could have any college guy she wanted.

Instead, they stayed in constant communication with texts and phone calls, often lasting for hours. He was so in love that he walked around with his head in a cloud that entire year. By going without lunches and eagerly working every chance for overtime, he was able to buy an engagement ring. When she agreed to become his wife, he was over the moon.

The next step was getting Grant's permission to marry his daughter. He wanted to do everything right, even if that meant losing Beth.

His heart was in his throat when he approached Grant. His father-in-law had asked a few questions, mainly about why Logan loved Beth, and he'd wanted to know about his future plans. Logan had nearly wept when Grant said he approved and gave the union his blessing.

Logan's attention was on the football game. The look Grant sent him messaged that he'd like for them to talk. Before he had a chance, however, Irene stepped out of the kitchen.

"Dinner's ready," Irene announced. He hadn't noticed that the food had been set on the table. Standing, he moved to the formal dining table and took his place next to Olivia, with Beth on the other side of their daughter.

"Can I say the blessing?" Olivia asked, looking to her grandpa for permission.

Grant smiled and nodded.

Everyone bowed their heads.

A Ferry Merry Christmas

"Thank you, God, for Christmas, and my iPad, and most of all for my daddy and mommy and my new sister or brother when the time is right and for Aunt Josie and Grandma and Grandpa and for sweet potatoes. Amen."

"Amen," Logan repeated, and caught Beth's gaze to find her smiling at the mention of a little brother or sister.

Over dinner, Logan didn't join in on the conversation, although he enjoyed the lively chatter that effortlessly flowed around the table. Beth's family recounted Christmases past and the years when the three Walsh siblings woke up at the crack of dawn, eager to open their gifts.

His childhood Christmases couldn't compare.

After a wonderful dinner, Logan helped with the dishes. He was about to go back to watching the football game when Grant asked him into the den.

This was it, he mused. Grant was going to read him the riot act, grill him about the past and the pain he'd caused Beth and Olivia. He'd want reassurances that Logan was sincere about moving back in with Beth and Olivia. Time to man up, he decided, and swallow his medicine.

Grant closed the door and gestured for Logan to sit

in the leather chair positioned in front of the wall-to-wall cherrywood bookcase. He walked over to the liquor cabinet and glanced over his shoulder.

"Brandy?" he asked.

Logan was about to automatically refuse, then changed his mind. He may well need alcohol to dull this ordeal. "Sure, thanks."

Filling each crystal snifter about an inch, he handed Logan one and then sat in an adjacent chair.

Stiffening, Logan waited for the talk-down.

Instead, Grant relaxed against the back of the leather chair, crossed his legs, and said, "It was good of you to join us for Christmas."

"I appreciate the welcome," Logan replied, and was sincere. He hadn't known what to expect. The hug from Irene had nearly brought tears to his eyes.

"I know why you asked to speak to me," he said, holding on to the snifter with both hands and leaning forward. He avoided eye contact.

"Oh?" The lone word was filled with curiosity.

"I made a huge mistake when I left Beth; I won't make excuses. I was wrong and I regret what I did."

"Actually, Logan, I wanted to apologize to you."

Certain he'd heard wrong, Logan jerked his head up. "Excuse me?"

"Irene and I should never have paid off Olivia's medical bills without discussing it with both of you first. We knew those expenses were a financial struggle with Beth no longer working. We thought we were helping."

"You did . . . You were." His throat grew tight. "I was a fool not to appreciate your generosity. For some crazy reason, I was convinced I'd failed Beth and Olivia and that they'd do better without me." His manhood had taken a hit, and fool that he was, he'd let pride nearly destroy the best thing that ever happened to him, and that was marrying Beth.

"My daughter loves you."

"I know," Logan agreed. "The thing is, I don't deserve her, and I know it. I thought she would be better off without me." That was the truth, the bottom line. Beth deserved so much more than anything he could offer her.

To his surprise, Grant chuckled. "Nothing could be further from the truth, son. I hope you know that."

Logan continued. "I don't know why you ever agreed to let a loser like me marry your daughter."

"You think you're a *loser*." Grant spit out the word like he would a lemon seed. "Is that the way you view yourself? My goodness, that explains a great deal. As for Beth choosing to marry you, you're dead wrong."

"I don't know what you mean."

Grant sipped his brandy. "Irene and I raised all three

of our children to be independent thinkers. If they made a mistake, we made sure they owned up to it. We didn't water down the consequences, either."

How he wished he'd been born into a family like this.

"Beth saw something in you few others had. She admired your determination to improve your situation with education and hard work. When you asked her to marry you with that ring, she understood the sacrifices you made to purchase the diamond and loved you even more for it. She believed in you; she still does."

"You understand, don't you? I didn't have anything to offer her when I asked her to be my wife, and have even less now."

"You love her, right?"

More than words would ever express. "Heart and soul. She could have married so much better than me."

"She wanted you. Irene and I approved of the union because we saw in you the same things our daughter did. You have grit, young man, and that's in short supply these days. Grit, determination, and a strong work ethic.

"I didn't exactly come from a pristine home myself. I enlisted in the Army the day after graduation to get away from a miserable home life. The Army taught me discipline. When my enlistment ran out, I had a clear idea of what I wanted in the future. I met Irene at a dance and was immediately drawn to her, the same way you felt when you met our Beth. I was strapped for funds, working nights and attending school, hoping to obtain a law degree. All while Irene stood by with support and love. Irene saw in me what Beth sees in you."

Logan hardly knew what to say. He had no idea Grant came from a dysfunctional family.

"I fully suspect that one day you'll run your own construction company. Yes, I know all about that, so don't look so surprised. Beth mentioned it shortly after you proposed."

Logan gasped. That had been his goal from the day he was first hired as a carpenter. He'd shared his dream with Beth, believing at the time it would be impossible. He half expected her to tell him to be more realistic. Instead, she'd encouraged him and had even suggested the name of his company: Dream Homes.

To his embarrassment, hearing about Grant's past, Logan felt tears leaking from his eyes. No one had ever believed in him like this, shown him this level of kindness. Certainly not anyone in his family.

"If that happens, me starting my own construction company, I'll be doing it after I repay you for the medical expenses you footed for Olivia's care."

Grant hesitated and then agreed. "As you wish."

A knock sounded against the door. "Dad?"

"Come in, Beth."

Grant shared a smile with Logan. "My daughter is worried I'm giving you the third degree."

Beth opened the door and paused as she anxiously glanced between Logan and her father. "Everything okay in here?" she asked.

"Never better," he answered, and clicked glasses with his father-in-law.

Beth relaxed. "Olivia fell asleep in front of the television and Josie wants to know if you'll play Monopoly with us."

Logan smiled. "Sure thing." He looked at Grant. "Are we done here, Dad?"

"We are, son. Merry Christmas."

Merry Christmas, indeed. And it was by far the best one of his life.

CHAPTER NINETEEN

"Are you sure this is where you want to spend Christmas Day?" Reed asked Avery. They stood in front of the Kirkland home of Kellie Stelter. Flecks of snow gently fell from the sky and the scent of pine mingled with the breeze. "What I mean to say is . . . I don't want you to give up our day together because you think it's what I want."

Avery couldn't keep from smiling. The minute she saw her brother with Kellie, she recognized the chemistry between them. The two couldn't take their eyes off each other the entire evening they'd spent together. It seemed while Harrison and Avery had been trapped on the ferry, her brother and Harrison's sister had gotten along like gangbusters.

Once off the ferry, they'd all enjoyed a dinner of roasted salmon, sourdough bread, asparagus, potatoes, and salad. Harrison and Avery had regaled them with the story of the birth of James's baby girl, which was their own bit of excitement. Their siblings had chatted nonstop about their own adventures, recalling the Christmas market and the ride on the Ferris wheel. Her brother had laughed when he recounted the mad rush to the ferry terminal only to learn it had been a false alarm.

Every few minutes Harrison would catch her eye and do his best to disguise his amusement. Avery was tickled herself. Clearly the two had enjoyed every minute they'd spent together.

It was after ten before Kellie suggested it was time for her to head home with Harrison. Avery could see her brother wanted to protest and probably would have if Kellie hadn't yawned. It had been a long day for all involved. Kellie's yawn had a rippling effect, and soon Avery was sleepy herself.

Standing at the door with her coat in hand, Kellie had turned back. "I had an idea . . . I know it's last-minute and all, but would you and Avery care to join us for Christmas dinner?"

Avery knew her brother well enough to realize she'd

be doing the shopping for their Christmas dinner. Everything her brother ate came from Uber Eats or was a frozen entrée. Brother and sister exchanged a look and it was quickly decided.

"We'd love it."

Avery was delighted by the invite.

"Great." Kellie's smile relayed how pleased she was.

Reed had the look of a boy anticipating opening gifts on Christmas morning.

Reed had walked Kellie and Harrison to the elevator while Avery remained behind. The condo was strangely silent after the lively dinner discussion. With them gone it felt as if all the air had left the room.

When Reed returned, he, too, seemed to feel how empty the condo was.

"By the way," Avery said, teasing her brother, "I have no objection to sharing our Christmas dinner with Harrison and Kellie."

Her brother's look was completely blank.

"You didn't give me the chance to answer earlier."

His brow furrowed as he seemed to be mentally reviewing the conversation. "I didn't? Are you sure?"

"Positive."

He rubbed the side of his face as if confused. "Sorry about that. You don't mind, do you?"

The original idea was supposed to be just the two of them and the traditions they'd shared with their grandmother. "It'll be fine," she assured him.

"Good." His shoulders sagged with relief.

Now, early Christmas afternoon, as they stood outside the car, her brother seemed to need reassurance.

"You like her, don't you?" Avery asked, although the answer was obvious.

"I do," Reed admitted. "Quite a lot, actually. You're okay spending it with Harrison?" His gaze held hers. "I know you're skeptical about dating someone in the military. I don't want you to be uncomfortable on my account."

"Stop, would you? I'm more than okay. Harrison's great." And he was. They'd exchanged texts several times over the last twenty-four hours. He hadn't pressured her into telling him her decision, and for that she was grateful. He had, however, made sure she understood how much he wanted the opportunity to see her again.

Tempted as she was, Avery remained unsure about whether getting involved with a man in the military was going to work, especially now that she knew he intended to make the Navy his career. Yet, even while aware of his plans, she'd been taken in by his wit and charm. She believed him when he assured her that he wasn't a player. She'd enjoyed the time on the ferry with him, exchanging banter, as they teased and joked with each other. There was something about Harrison that was hard to resist. Even the way he sensed her hesitation and patiently worked reminded her of his interest.

The kiss they'd exchanged after Noelle's birth certainly complicated her decision. She recognized the attraction between Reed and Kellie because it looked just like what she was experiencing with Harrison. An attraction that strong was difficult to ignore. Her biggest fear was knowing that if they did become involved, it would mean long absences while he was at sea. Depending on his mission, there would be a complete lack of any communication. If anything were to happen, she wouldn't know for weeks on end. That uncertainty gave her pause.

Avery didn't know how those left behind lived, knowing the ones they loved and cared deeply about were in constant danger. Having basically lost everyone important in her life, other than Reed, Avery remained leery and yet . . .

"Hey, you two, what's the holdup? In case you didn't notice, it's snowing. Come inside." Kellie stood on the porch wearing a Santa hat and gestured for them to enter the house. The front door was decorated with a festive evergreen wreath with a large red bow and silver bells.

"Shall we?" Reed asked, glancing away from Kellie long enough to focus on Avery.

"Merry Christmas," Avery called out as she started toward Kellie. Harrison stood behind his sister.

Leading the way up the steps, Avery hugged Kellie and then briefly Harrison. She saw the disappointment in his eyes when she broke free.

She paused just inside the entry. Kellie's home was lovely. Her eyes went to the flocked Christmas tree, placed close to the picture window. It was decorated with silver and blue ornaments.

Reed followed her carrying a large poinsettia and a bottle of RumChata. Avery loved that he chose the RumChata, as it was their grandparents' favorite and a Christmas tradition. After their grandfather passed, Grams continued the tradition. The flavored alcoholic drink was a special treat both Avery and Reed waited for each Christmas evening. Having him include it in their celebration was his way of continuing the tradition in memory of their precious grandmother.

When Avery walked into the living area, the first thing that greeted her was the aroma of the turkey roasting in the oven. It smelled delicious. She'd had a light breakfast of toast and coffee, wanting to save her appetite for dinner. Her stomach growled in anticipation of the meal they were about to enjoy.

Harrison was at her side and helped Avery remove her coat, his hands lingering on her shoulders. "I can't tell you how happy I am that you're here."

"I'm happy, too," she said, and briefly placed her hand over his, letting him know she truly meant it.

While he hung her wool coat in the hall closet, Kellie and Reed had disappeared into the kitchen. A poinsettia sat beneath the Christmas tree, along with a few opened gifts still in their boxes.

"Come sit with me," Harrison said, and reached for Avery's hand. He led her to the sofa across from the fireplace, where a gentle fire flickered. The room was warm and cozy. She noticed the dining room table was already set with a white linen tablecloth. It looked like Kellie had used her best dishes along with crystal wineglasses.

"I couldn't wait to see you," Harrison said, keeping hold of her hand. Before she could comment, he added, "I know it's only been a little more than forty-eight hours, but it felt like much, much longer." He hesitated and looked unsure, his gaze drifting away from her as if he was carefully considering his words.

"Am I coming on too strong?" he asked.

Avery rather enjoyed his lack of confidence. It told her he understood her concerns and took them seriously. "No. The truth is, I was anxious to see you again, too."

"Does this mean you'd be willing to spend more time together? I know it isn't technically after Christmas, but close enough, right?" He rushed the words together, as if he didn't say them fast enough, she might change her mind.

"Well . . ."

"Don't say no. I realize you have a few qualms about dating me, and I can appreciate everything you've said. I can't deny that I'll be away for lengthy periods of time, and that's difficult for any relationship. I'm not asking you to date me exclusively, although that's what I'd like. It's too soon, but . . ." He paused again and heaved a sigh before he continued as though concerned he'd blown it.

"I'm making a mess of this, aren't I?"

He was so endearing it was difficult to find fault with anything he'd said. "I'm thinking I'd like to get to know you better. We can take this slow and easy and see how things develop."

"Does that mean you'd go to the movies with me this weekend?"

She hesitated, as if this were a weighty question. "Do you know what's playing?"

"No. I don't really care, as long as you're with me." He exhaled as though upset with himself. "I'm doing it again, aren't I?"

She raised her brows, questioning him.

"Being overly eager," he supplied.

Avery reached for her phone.

Harrison watched her closely, his forehead creased with a frown. "What are you doing?"

"Checking the listings for the movies."

"Does that mean you'd be willing to go?"

She glanced up and nodded. "There's an action movie with Tom Cruise and a romantic comedy, too. Which one do you prefer?"

"Either. Both," he said.

"Hey, you two," Kellie said, coming out from the kitchen. "The turkey is out of the oven."

Avery rushed to her feet. "Oh my goodness, I should be helping with dinner." She felt terrible that she had left Kellie with all the work preparing their meal.

"No need," Reed said, carrying a large platter with the turkey. He set it in the middle of the table. "Kellie and I have got everything dished up and ready to serve."

"I apologize." Avery was embarrassed by her bad manners.

"No apology necessary. Harrison asked for a few minutes so he could speak to you alone, and . . ."

"Kell," Harrison protested and rolled his eyes.

"Did you?" Avery enjoyed teasing him.

"It worked out perfectly," Reed interjected. "I wanted a few minutes alone with Kellie, too."

"Avery and I are going to the movies this weekend," Harrison announced as he pulled out a chair for her to take a seat. He caught Kellie's eye and winked.

She winked back and smiled at Avery.

Reed stood behind Kellie's chair, then took his own. Before they ate, the four joined hands and Reed said a short prayer.

"Grams would have loved meeting both of you," Avery said as they passed around the dishes. She loaded her plate with mashed potatoes and giblet gravy. She skipped the green beans and took an extra scoop of stuffing, her favorite. She noticed Harrison did the same, passing over the vegetable in favor of extra stuffing. By the time they finished with all the side dishes, her plate was full to overflowing.

Their meal was wonderful as they exchanged banter, joking back and forth. From the way they interacted, it was as if they'd known one another far longer than they had. Avery had been convinced this first

Christmas without her grandmother would be hard as she and Reed tried to make the best of it alone together. And yet here she was enjoying herself just the way their grandmother would have wanted.

Afterwards the four worked together cleaning the kitchen. Kellie insisted on packaging up several containers of leftovers, claiming everything tasted even better the second day.

"I doubt that's possible," Reed said. "I can't remember a meal I enjoyed more, or the company."

Once everything had been set right in the kitchen, Harrison suggested they watch a Christmas movie.

"How about *Die Hard*?" Reed said. "That's one of my favorites."

"That's not a Christmas movie," Avery argued. "What about *Home Alone*?"

Reed rolled his eyes. "How many times have you watched that silly movie? A dozen?"

"Probably more. It's tradition," Avery argued.

Reed wasn't listening. "What's your choice?" he asked Kellie.

Harrison's sister shared a smile with Avery. "*Home Alone*."

"No, please, no."

"Don't I get a say?" Harrison asked.

In a united chorus, the three others said, "No."

"Okay, okay, it's *Home Alone*," Harrison said with a laugh as he reached for the remote.

Reed and Kellie claimed the sofa. Kellie snuggled up against Reed and he placed his arm around her shoulders and kissed the top of her head.

Harrison reached for Avery's hand and the two nestled in the loveseat as the movie started to play.

Although Avery had watched the movie many times, it never failed to make her laugh. She enjoyed being close to Harrison and didn't object when he tucked his arm around her. With her stomach full of their meal, she rested her head against his shoulder and yawned at the end of the movie.

When the last of the credits rolled across the screen, Reed sat up and announced, "It's time for the RumChata."

"It's a Christmas tradition that started with our grandparents," Avery explained.

"This is our first Christmas without our grandmother. It seems fitting for us to continue in her honor," Reed added.

Kellie brought out four small shot glasses and set them on the coffee table. Reed opened the bottle and poured each of them two knuckles. He distributed the glasses and then raised his in a toast.

"To Grams."

"To Grams," Avery repeated.

Kellie and Harrison echoed the toast and raised their glasses.

They each took a small taste.

"Not bad," Harrison said, arching his brows. "This is one Christmas tradition I wouldn't mind continuing. I imagine you miss her," he said, looking at Avery.

"Nothing feels the same. I dreaded this first Christmas without her, unsure how Reed and I would get through it. I was afraid there would be this giant hole with her gone. For the last several years it's only been the three of us."

"How do you feel now?" Reed asked, catching her eye.

"Today, you mean?" Avery asked after a thoughtful moment. "It feels different and at the same time perfect. What about you?" she asked her brother.

He stared down at the glass in his hand. "This might sound a little silly, but I'm going to say it anyway. I think Grams might have been behind the four of us meeting the way we did. I'm convinced she meant for us to share this day together."

"I think you're right," Avery agreed, then sipped her drink in Grams's honor. "That would be just like her." Deep down, Avery knew their grandmother would know how terribly they would miss her this Christmas and would work from heaven to make this day special.

"It's too much of a coincidence that the four of us would meet up the way we did," Reed added. "I mean, what are the odds that Harrison and Avery would find each other on the ferry with literally hundreds of passengers on board."

"And that the two of us would happen upon each other," Kellie added. She reached for Reed's hand.

"Normally I would have been on the East Coast, spending Christmas with my parents," Harrison said.

"Our parents, who decided to take a cruise this year instead," Kellie inserted.

"That's a fair amount of finagling," Harrison said, sounding skeptical.

Reed and Avery laughed in unison.

"I wish I had known your Grams," Kellie said, her fingers entwined with Reed's. "Having met the two of you, I suspect she must have been a special woman."

"She was," Avery agreed. Looking toward the heavens, she raised her glass to Grams, her heart filled with love.

EPILOGUE

One Year Later

"Welcome, welcome." Lilly Jordan opened the door for Avery and Harrison.

"Sorry we're late," Avery apologized. They'd gotten caught up in a snarled traffic jam on their way to celebrate Noelle Rose's first birthday.

"Noelle is just about to eat her cake," James called from the kitchen. "We're waiting to sing first."

Noelle sat in her high chair in the dining room. A spoon was in her hand, which she banged against the tray, excited with all the company and the fuss. A buffet table held several beautifully wrapped birthday gifts. Avery added her and Harrison's contribution to the collection.

"Your timing is perfect," Lilly assured them.

The first person Avery recognized was Virginia.

"Virginia," she greeted her, and was about to give her a hug when the woman said, "I'm Veronica. Virginia is getting the paper plates."

"You're not Virginia?" Harrison asked when it was clear this was an identical twin.

"No one has ever been able to tell us apart," Virginia called out from the other room.

"Even our parents," Veronica added. "I insisted on crashing this party since my generous sister gave away my Christmas cookies last year."

"Oh, hush," Virginia teased. "We both know it was never about those cookies."

Veronica shrugged good-naturedly. "She's right, you know. It really wasn't about those silly cookies."

Avery's attention was sidetracked by Olivia, who stood next to her parents. Logan had his arm around Beth's waist. His gaze was on his wife, and the tenderness that shone in his eyes was enough to make Avery smile. The love that had brought them back together was real and strong.

"Can we have the cake now?" Olivia asked, clearly eager for the dessert.

"Olivia," her father gently chastised. "It's impolite to ask."

Covering her mouth with both hands, Olivia mumbled, "Oops. Sorry."

"We need to wait to sing 'Happy Birthday' first," James explained just as the doorbell rang again. He excused himself and headed for the front of the house.

"I'm going to be a big sister," Olivia announced. "I asked for a sister, but daddy explained that I'll be just as happy with a little brother." She shrugged as if this was yet to be decided.

"Congratulations," Avery said. She was pleased for Beth, who glowed with happiness.

"Thanks. We're excited. It seems everything is happening at once. Logan is working and taking business classes and I'm teaching first grade. Our lives are busy and full. We couldn't be happier about this baby."

"When are you due?"

"Not until October," she said.

Liam and Suzie, two of the people from the band, entered the dining room, calling out their hellos and Merry Christmases to everyone. Liam carried his guitar.

"Now?" Olivia asked, looking at her parents.

Liam brought the guitar out of the case and lifted the strap over his shoulder. He strummed a few chords before starting the birthday song. They all joined in, and baby Noelle watched with glee, her eyes bright with excitement. The spoon made repeated raps against the tray as she was serenaded.

Lilly served the cake, and they sat around the dining room table and caught up with one another since last year, when they'd spent that fateful day together.

"So," James said, eyeing Avery and Harrison. "Are you two . . . together?"

"We're dating," Harrison supplied, and looked at Avery with a look in his eyes that warmed her heart each and every time.

"Exclusively," she added.

He reached for Avery's hand and gave it a gentle squeeze. "There's no one else for me."

"Or me," she whispered, holding Harrison's eyes.

Liam and Suzie updated them about the band's latest bookings and issued an invitation for the New Year's Eve party they were playing. "We got free tickets as part of the arrangement. I hope you can all join us."

"We'd love to," Harrison said, and looked to Avery for agreement. They hadn't made any special plans beyond Christmas.

"That sounds great."

After thirty minutes, Harrison glanced at the time. "I hate to eat and run. Avery and I are meeting our siblings for lunch at Anthony's."

"No problem. You mentioned you couldn't stay long when you responded to the invitation," James said, and escorted them to the door.

Once outside, they hurried down the steps. "It was great to see everyone," Avery said.

"Did you get what Virginia was saying about the cookies?"

"Yup. I'll explain it later."

"What I can't believe is how identical they are."

They chatted all the way to the waterfront, remembering the connections they'd made that fateful day. By the time they arrived, Reed and Kellie had already been seated. The hostess led them to the table.

Reed and Kellie sat next to each other, their fingers clasped. That was when Avery noticed the diamond on Kellie's hand. Her brother had done it. He'd asked Kellie to be his wife and she'd agreed.

They both looked up when Avery and Harrison approached. "I see congratulations are in order," Avery said, and hugged Kellie's shoulders.

Kellie's eyes were bright with joy.

"Have you set a date?" Avery asked, as Harrison pulled out her chair for her to take a seat next to his sister.

"June, I think. It'll take that long to get everything organized."

"I suggested a Valentine's wedding," Reed said. "I had no idea weddings took months and months of planning."

"They do," Kellie reiterated. "But I promise the wait will be worth it."

The server approached the table for their drink order. "Did you hear?" she asked, looking out over Puget Sound.

"Hear?" Harrison asked.

"It's happened again. Another ferry is stalled halfway between Bainbridge Island and Seattle."

Avery and Harrison locked gazes and smiled.

"I wonder," Avery said, "if those passengers know how lucky they are."

ABOUT THE AUTHOR

DEBBIE MACOMBER is a leading voice in women's fiction. Fifteen of her novels have reached #1 on the *New York Times* bestseller lists, and six of her beloved Christmas novels have been made into hit movies on the Hallmark Channel, in addition to the original series *Debbie Macomber's Cedar Cove,* based on Macomber's Cedar Cove books. There are more than 200 million copies of her books in print worldwide.

debbiemacomber.com
Facebook.com/debbiemacomberworld
X: @debbiemacomber
Instagram: @debbiemacomber
Pinterest.com/macomberbooks

Also by #1 *New York Times* bestselling author
DEBBIE MACOMBER

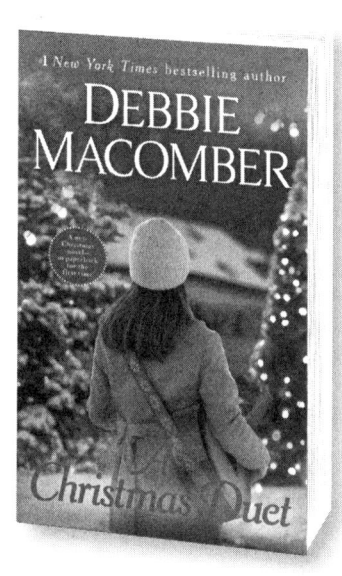

Savor the magic of the season with
Debbie Macomber's romantic Christmas novels,
filled with warmth, humor, the promise of love,
and a dash of unexpected adventure.

Visit DebbieMacomber.com

BALLANTINE BOOKS

FROM #1 *NEW YORK TIMES* BESTSELLING AUTHOR

DEBBIE MACOMBER

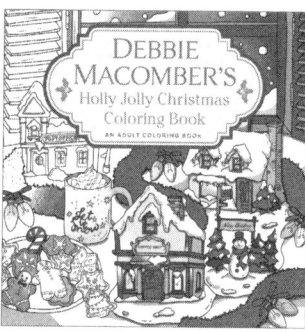

Enchanting adult coloring books from the
queen of Christmas stories, featuring all-new festive
illustrations inspired by her treasured holiday novels

Visit DebbieMacomber.com

BALLANTINE BOOKS

2-in-1 collections from #1 *New York Times* bestselling author

DEBBIE MACOMBER

Sign up for Debbie's newsletter at
DebbieMacomber.com

BALLANTINE BOOKS

NOW IN PAPERBACK
from #1 *New York Times* bestselling author

DEBBIE MACOMBER

Debbie Macomber's books offer inspiring stories about friendship, reinvention, and hope. These stories affirm the ability of every woman to forge a new path, believe in love, and fearlessly find happiness.

Sign up for Debbie's newsletter
at DebbieMacomber.com

BALLANTINE BOOKS